Cowboy to the Core

JOANNA WAYNE

All the characters in this book have no existence outside the imagination of the author, and have no relation whatsoever to anyone bearing the same name or names. They are not even distantly inspired by any individual known or unknown to the author, and all the incidents are pure invention.

First published in Great Britain 2010
Large Print edition 2010
Harlequin Mills & Boon Limited,
Eton House, 18-24 Paradise Road,
Richmond, Surrey TW9 1SR

ISBN: 978 0 263 22158 9

Harlequin Mills & Boon policy is to use papers that are natural, renewable and recyclable products and made from wood grown in sustainable forests. The logging and manufacturing process conform to the legal environmental regulations of the country of origin.

Printed and bound in Great Britain
by CPI Antony Rowe, Chippenham, Wiltshire

JOANNA WAYNE

was born and raised in Shreveport, Louisiana, and received her undergraduate and graduate degrees from LSU-Shreveport. She moved to New Orleans in 1984, and it was there that she attended her first writing class and joined her first professional writing organisation. Her first novel, *Deep in the Bayou*, was published in 1994.

Now, dozens of published books later, Joanna has made a name for herself as being on the cutting edge of romantic suspense in both series and single-title novels. She has been on the Waldenbooks bestseller list for romance and has won many industry awards. She is a popular speaker at writing organisations and local community functions and has taught creative writing at the University of New Orleans Metropolitan College.

She currently resides in a small community forty miles north of Houston, Texas, with her husband. Though she still has many family and emotional ties to Louisiana, she loves living in the Lone Star State. You may write to Joanna at P.O. Box 265, Montgomery, Texas 77356.

To my good friend
and golfing buddy, Sharon,
who spent a marvelous day with me
at the Renaissance Festival
and took dozens of pictures to
help capture the sights and spirit of
the exciting event. We had a blast!
And an apology to the handsome,
skilled and no doubt noble jousters
who entertained us so magnificently.
Their performance was
the highlight of the day.

Prologue

The woman's voluminous skirt and layers of petticoats swished about her ankles. Her auburn hair was piled on top of her head, loose curls dancing about her cheeks and wispy tendrils escaping down the back of her neck.

A queen, dressed for a coronation ball, her jade velvet bodice trimmed in exquisite white lace that edged her cleavage. Or perhaps not royalty, but a courtesan with seductive wiles to please and excite the king's men.

A knight stepped into view. The air became

electric as the two turned to face each other. The woman's eyes were blazing but shadowed with fear. The man's expression was hidden beneath the metallic armor that shielded his head and face, yet an aura of evil surrounded him. He moved toward her.

She tried to back away, but there was no time. In one quick movement, he pulled an ivory-handled dagger from the sheath at his side and aimed the point of the long, slender blade at the woman's heart.

The woman's scream penetrated the night as a rush of crimson spilled onto the white lace and pooled in the rich green fabric of her blouson.

Choking, Dani forced herself to the woman's aid. Their gazes locked, and Dani's blood ran cold.

The cinnamon-brown eyes staring back at her were her own.

Dani Baxter jerked to sitting position, her breathing sharp, painful gasps and her pulse racing. She was fully awake now, but the images remained seared into her brain. Everything had seemed so real.

Her psychic experiences appeared as a dream at times, but this couldn't have been one. Not only did she not know the people but they weren't even from this century. The telepathic connection would be pointless since she could do nothing to change the situation. Her infrequent visions never worked that way.

It was just a nightmare, no doubt brought on by fatigue and the countless hours she'd spent looking at spring formal wear lines in New York last week. Work-related stress. It happened to everyone. It didn't mean a thing, yet her breath continued to sting as if she were outside on a frigid morning.

She was overreacting. She hadn't had one of the dreaded visions in more than a year. And she'd never had one as violent as this.

She checked the clock. 2:00 a.m. She needed sleep and water. Her throat felt parched.

Tossing back the sheet, she threw her legs over the side of the bed and ground her bare feet against the chilly slats of the polished hardwood floors. She tiptoed past her daughter's door so as not to wake her and padded down the stairs to the second-floor kitchen of the town house.

The dream continued to haunt her. It was the eyes, she decided. They'd thrown her, but the woman hadn't been her. The face had never registered, and the hair was definitely different. The nightmare woman's was a deep auburn, long enough to pile on top of her head. It was curly as well. Dani's hair was brown, with just a touch of copper highlights. Even those came from the salon. And she wore it in a chin-length bob, professional-looking and easy to manage.

So get over it and get some sleep. No

marauding knight in full armor is going to plunge a dagger into a woman's chest in my swank downtown complex.

Dani drank her water and went back to her crisp sheets and plump pillows. Tomorrow would be another very busy day at Duran Muton, and there was a PTA meeting tomorrow night. She needed her rest. And for the woman in green to quietly slip back in time.

Chapter One

One month later

"Mom, may I invite Katie for a sleepover tomorrow night?"

"Katie came for a sleepover last Saturday night."

"What's that got to do with it?"

"Nothing, I suppose. I just thought you and I might go out to dinner tomorrow evening and catch a movie."

"Katie could go with us. There's a cool new comedy that we're dying to see."

Dani truly hated comedies unless they were liberally sprinkled with romance. “Go ahead and invite her. We’ll go to dinner, and then I’ll drop you two off at the cinema.”

“Thanks, Mom.” Celeste rewarded Dani’s acquiescence with a quick hug. “You’re the greatest.”

But not so great that her preteen daughter wanted to spend time with her. Dani went back to cleaning off her desk. She kept on top of everything at work, but she tended to let the non-urgent home office duties slide until they threatened to overflow their boundaries.

She slit open the next envelope—an application for a credit card that claimed to do everything except pay itself. She fed it into the shredder and picked up a postcard inviting her to an open house for a new day spa. She scanned it and dropped it into file thirteen. She did the same with a donation request from a charity she’d never heard of.

Which left a gold-bordered envelope staring her in the face. Cripes! The wedding invitation. She'd meant to send her regrets to Bethany Sue weeks ago.

Oh, well, the bride-to-be had probably figured out by now she wasn't coming. Bethany might already be married and heading for divorce court if this union followed the way of her first two marriages.

She pulled the invitation from the envelope. There were two silhouettes in the muted background. A woman in a flowing Elizabethan gown. A knight in full armor.

Dani's heart slammed against the walls of her chest as the images from her murderous dream came back to haunt her in vivid details. The rich green of the fabric. The crimson pool of blood.

Get a hold of yourself, Dani Baxter. It was only a stupid nightmare.

She swallowed hard and read the invitation. The nuptials joining Bethany Sue Graves and Arnold Pickering would be celebrated at the Texas Renaissance Festival in Plantersville, Texas.

Dani checked the date. This Sunday. Two days away. The ceremony was at ten in the morning, but there was to be a prewedding dinner celebration on the festival grounds tomorrow night. The reply card said regrets only.

Regrets only? No one did that, especially when there was a dinner involved. Well, no one except Bethany Sue. She'd always followed a different drummer. Actually, she usually followed the sax player.

Dani and Bethany had been friends from seventh grade through high school. Bethany had been one of the few girls at their junior high who didn't make Dani feel like a freak because her grandmother was a known psychic. At one time they'd been as close as Celeste and her friend Katie were now. They'd shared too many secrets and important moments to count.

They seldom communicated now except for an occasional e-mail or quick phone call. Their lives had gone in vastly different directions. Still, it would be great to see her again—just not this weekend. There was nothing to do but try to reach her by phone and apologize for forgetting to send her regrets in a timely manner.

Dropping the invitation back to the pile, Dani pulled out her cell phone, found Bethany's number and pushed the call button. Bethany answered on the third ring, the excitement spilling into her hello.

"Is that wedding jitters I hear?"

"Dani, where are you? Arnie and I were just talking about you. He can't wait to meet you. And, no, there's not a jitter in my body."

Which just went to show how naive Bethany still was after two failed marriages. "Great. I couldn't be happier for you. Does Arnie know how lucky he is?"

"He must. I tell him all the time. So where are you?"

"In Austin. I'm afraid I've committed a terrible social faux pas. I should have called as soon as I got the invitation, and, unfortunately, I just realized the reply specified regrets only."

"And in your case regrets are not acceptable. I can't get married without you here."

"I'd love to be there, but I can't possibly make it this weekend. Celeste has plans and…"

"Celeste will willingly cancel her plans. Did you not even read the note I stuck in the envelope with your invitation?"

Actually she hadn't even seen the note. She turned the envelope upside down, and the note and accompanying map fell out.

"You must bring Celeste. She'll love the festival and the party. There will be mimes and jesters and all sorts of courtly entertainment.

And, like I said in the note, bring a date, as well. You can even let Celeste bring a friend. The more the merrier."

"I'm not dating anyone, and I haven't made reservations. I doubt I could even get a room in…" She checked the invitation again. "In Plantersville." Wherever that was.

"There aren't any places to stay in Plantersville. It's a tiny, rural town. But they just had a cancellation at the bed-and-breakfast near Magnolia where we're staying. If you call right now, you can get it.

"You will so love the place, Dani. Weather permitting, they serve breakfast on this magnificent veranda. The phone number is on the back of the map I sent you along with that of some motels in The Woodlands."

"I really wish I could be there, but…"

"No excuses. You simply have to come. And it's good you're not bringing a date. I have this terrific man I want you to meet."

Dani groaned. "That is not a selling point." Still, a weekend getaway to a Renaissance festival might be fun for her and Celeste. And she did hate to disappoint Bethany Sue.

She did a quick study of the enclosed map. The festival grounds were a few miles off Highway 105, northwest of Houston, probably a good three-hour drive from Austin. "What time is the party tomorrow night?"

"Eight, but come early in the day. You'll want time to enjoy the festival. There's so much to see and do."

"Exactly what does one wear to a Renaissance wedding?"

"Something incredibly sexy and fit for a queen's ball in the Elizabethan period. But don't worry, you can buy or rent outfits at the festival. Men's, women's and children's, so you don't have to pack a thing."

An Elizabethan ball gown. She didn't need this now.

"So can I count on you?" Bethany pleaded.

Dani swallowed hard. Being a covert psychic was bad enough. Letting a nightmare dictate her life was sick. "Okay, we'll be there."

Now who was afraid of a big, bad dream?

MARCUS ABBOT TUGGED HIS weathered work Stetson a bit lower on his forehead. "Care to repeat that, Cutter Martin, 'cause I could have sworn you just said you want me to babysit a couple of spoiled Hollywood brats."

"Just for a day. Lance Harper is in Houston filming a new movie, and he needs a bodyguard for his two daughters while they're attending the Renaissance festival. It's just down the road. You've probably seen the ads for it around town."

"I've seen the propaganda." Marcus leaned against the fence post and stared down the snorting bull on the other side of the barbed wire. "This is not the kind of work I signed on for."

"It's protection," Cutter said. "That's what our name says. Investigation and Protection."

"Nothing in there about babysitting." And nothing like the assignment he and Cutter Martin had just completed. They'd gone into Mexico and located and rescued a teenage girl who'd disappeared while on vacation with her family.

Turned out she'd been kidnapped and was being sold into sexual slavery. Bringing her home safely had rivaled the exhilaration of completing a successful mission as a Navy SEAL. Babysitting Lance Harper's kids while they played in a historic playground wouldn't.

But Marcus wasn't a naval commando anymore. He might as well get used to that. He missed the military life a lot more than he'd expected, but he had a new goal. And if it took babysitting to reach it, so be it. Besides, a man couldn't ask for a better boss than Cutter.

"So when do I acquire the Hollywood horrors?"

"Not until next Saturday, but since the festival is only open on weekends, I figured you'd want to tour the grounds by yourself this weekend to get the lay of the land."

Marcus nodded. That was a definite. He'd never go out on assignment without adequate fact gathering. His mind jumped back to the mission he'd faced just before he'd finished his last tour of duty. Men's sweat and fetid earth had clogged his nostrils. Danger had hung in the heavy air like a blanket of oppressive smoke. He'd always had a sixth sense for danger. That night was no exception.

He shook his mind to clear it before he became lost in the past. "Is that it?"

"Yeah, except that Linney wants to know if you'll join us for dinner tonight."

"Pasta?"

Cutter laughed. "How'd you guess?"

Easy. It was practically the only thing she could cook. Well, that and canned soup. Not that Cutter cared. The guy was so in love with his new wife that he lit up like a round of firepower when she walked into the room.

Marcus had known that feeling once. It had turned on him and bitten him in the… No. Who was he kidding? He'd never had the kind of relationship Cutter and Linney had. Not much chance he ever would after the way his ex had stomped him into the mud.

Horses and cattle. Maybe even a good dog. Those were things you could count on. That was one of the real advantages of working for Cutter. When they weren't on duty for the company, they worked on his ranch, the Double M.

"If that's it, I'll go back to hauling hay."

"That's it." Cutter swatted at a worrisome horsefly. "I'll go with you. Got to work up a pasta appetite by seven."

ODORS OF FUNNEL CAKES, roasting meats and frying fish and chips greeted them the moment they stepped from their car among dozens of other arriving festival patrons. Dani's mouth watered in spite of the pastries and coffee they'd stopped for en route.

Celeste and Katie hurried ahead of her, their tennis shoes kicking up dust along the well-traveled path that maneuvered among row upon row of parked cars and pickup trucks.

The air sparked with chatter, laughter and an electric excitement among the festival goers, many dressed in elaborate costumes.

They were greeted at the gate by a jovial, middle-aged man dressed in a short red and green skirt over tights. From his looks, he might have ushered them into the king's court a century ago. Dani was starting to catch the spirit in spite of her earlier reservations.

Once inside what appeared to be the city walls, activity increased dramatically, and her imagination was spurred by the line of fascinating shops and concessions and the number of people in creative costumes. Old England had never had it so good.

Weirdly, she had a strange tingle of anticipation dancing inside her as if something big was going to happen to her this weekend. Maybe Bethany's friend would turn out to be a winner.

Forget it. There wasn't a man alive who could tolerate a woman psychic for long, and she would not put herself and Celeste through another divorce to prove that point.

She hurried to keep up with the girls, then slowed to gawk at a voluptuous young woman bulging out of an outfit that consisted mostly of chain mail. The woman posed for a whiskered guy in an Astros cap who was all but salivating as he snapped her picture.

Dani turned to catch sight of Katie and Celeste walking toward a nearby dress shop. They sashayed past a hunky cowboy and disappeared inside. The guy looked out of place. Not because of his worn jeans, scuffed boots and black Stetson. After all, this was Texas. But the recalcitrant grimace on his craggy face made it clear he wasn't joining in the revelry that surrounded him.

He looked up and caught her staring at him. An unwelcome burn crept to her cheeks as he tipped his hat and traded the frown for a devastating smile. Oh, well, he was probably used to females admiring his blatant virility.

Head high and looking straight ahead, she strode right past him. She followed the sound of girls' giggling to the back of the shop. Celeste was holding up a low-cut sapphire-blue gown. The padded cups at the top of the lacing could hold a set of double Ds. Celeste had trouble filling out her training bra.

"You're a little too young to go the wench route," Dani said.

"You could wear it, Ms. Baxter," Katie said. "You'd be hot!"

"We're going to a wedding, not a bawdry

bash." At least she hoped that was the case; Dani had traded hot for sophisticated several years ago, at the same time she'd swapped her cheating husband for single parenthood and a position with Duran Muton.

"How about these?" Dani said, moving to a rack of pastel-hued, ankle-length dresses with puffy sleeves and high-buttoned necklines.

Celeste scrunched her nose as if she smelled a skunk. "I'd look like a kid."

"You are a kid."

"Ooh, look at this," Katie called, her gaze riveted on a handkerchief-layered skirt of various hues of blue and green, topped with a white peasant blouse. It hung on the highest rack, slightly out of reach.

A youthful clerk dressed in knee-high black boots, tights and a clingy, crimson blouson appeared from between the garment racks. Hooking the hanger, she retrieved the outfit so they could get a better look.

"We're attending a dinner tonight on the grounds and a Renaissance wedding tomorrow morning," Dani explained. "Do you have any suggestions as to what would be considered appropriate attire?"

"Just about anything from the period will go for the dinner. People get very daring and inventive at those affairs. But fairies, definitely fairies for the girls for the wedding. You're both so petite. You'll be adorable nymphs."

"Adorable?" Celeste groaned.

"You just uttered the kiss of death," Dani said.

The clerk took a step backward and gave Dani a studied once-over. "I have just the dress for you for the wedding."

"Nothing too revealing," Dani said as the clerk hurried away.

Celeste and Katie moved to the rack of fairy dresses, airy confections that came with their own silver wings. Dani sneaked a peek at a cherry-red blouson with exquisite embroidered details, topped by a black leather bustier pulled so tight it was almost as if the big-breasted mannequin didn't have a waist.

Incredibly sexy. Probably similar to what the cowboy's girlfriend was trying on while he waited outside. One glimpse of her in that would no doubt wipe the grimace right off his handsome, tanned face.

Impulsively, she scanned the area. The cowboy was nowhere in sight. Irritated at herself for giving the guy a second thought, she went back to perusing a rack of dresses. She held one up in front of the floor-length mirror. Over her shoulder she caught a reflection of a nice-looking man in a blue knit shirt who seemed to be staring at her from around the sexy mannequin.

For a second, she thought he was one of the reps she did business with. On second glance, she realized he wasn't. His hair was not only darker but he had a lot more of it than the rep.

She hung the dress back on the rack and moved on until she heard the clerk's voice.

"I practically had to pluck it from a customer's hands, but she didn't have the figure to wear it anyway. You'll be a knockout in it."

Dani turned. Her pulse quickened. Her knees went weak. The luscious frock in the clerk's hands was almost a dead second for the green gown from her nightmare.

"Is something wrong? Are you ill?"

The clerk's voice floated above her, distorted by a thick fog that clouded Dani's mind. Slowly the haze cleared, and the attacking images became sharp and chilling. She struggled to breathe.

"Move back. Give her air."

Her gaze sought out the voice. The cowboy. She reached out to him as her body crumpled, and she sank into a bloody river of darkness.

Chapter Two

Marcus knelt beside the fallen woman and felt her pulse. It was slow but not in the danger zone. Her eyes fluttered open, and her gaze met his. A heated jolt galloped up his spine. A weird reaction to a woman he'd never met, even one as attractive as this. It had to be the haunted shadows in the depths of her big brown eyes.

"Are you a doctor?" someone asked.

"I'm a combat medic." He turned to the crowd. "Stand back a bit. She needs air."

The hovering bystanders retreated a few

inches as two young girls pushed through them. "Mom! What happened?"

"It's okay, Celeste. I'm fine." The woman's voice was uneven, and she swayed when she tried to get up.

"Whoa, there," Marcus said, reaching out to steady her. "Take it slow."

"Did you fall?" the other girl questioned.

"She passed out," someone volunteered.

Another onlooker pointed her finger at Marcus. "He's a combat medic, trained on the battlefield. He knows what he's doing."

The woman was standing now, and she shook loose of Marcus's protective grasp. "I just fainted," she insisted. "Believe me, I'm fine."

Maybe, but from what Marcus had seen, that wasn't the full story. He'd been looking right at her—okay, checking her out—when the clerk had brushed by him and held up a long green dress for the woman to admire.

Instead her face had twisted into the kind of

agonizing pain he'd seen on soldiers when they'd taken a direct hit. Not the kind of reaction one would expect from a woman eyeballing a ball gown in a Renaissance festival shop.

"You should at least let me check your pulse again," Marcus said.

"Yeah," the girl who'd called her "Mom" agreed. "He's a medic. That's practically a doctor."

"I don't need a doctor or a medic, Celeste. My pulse is terrific."

She tossed her head and looked around as if searching for the nearest escape route. When she spotted the exit, she started toward it.

The girls followed her. Marcus tagged along behind them, though he wasn't sure why. He didn't usually chase after women who were trying to avoid him, but then he seldom met one who hotwired his spine the way this one had. Actually, that was probably a reason to run the other way. But then his buddies in the SEALs had always said he was a danger junkie.

Once they were outside the shop, the woman pulled a tissue from her pocket and dabbed away the beads of sweat that had formed on her forehead.

"Are you sure you're okay, Mom?"

"I'm certain."

"Well, then why did you faint?" the other girl asked.

"Good point," Marcus added.

She glared at him, her brows raised as if questioning why he was still hanging around. "Low blood sugar."

"Since when do you have problems with blood sugar?" Celeste protested. "You sometimes go all day without eating."

"Well, I'm hungry now," she said, obviously trying to dismiss her daughter's concern. "We should have lunch and choose our dresses for the party later."

So the woman was lying about her medical condition, but something had happened to make her fade to black—or rather to a ghostly white—back there. None of his business, he told himself. He didn't listen.

"Food sounds good," Marcus said. "How about I join you? That way I'll be there in case your blood sugar level doesn't regulate quickly enough and you require medical assistance."

Her face reddened as if she knew he'd caught her in the lie. Still, she didn't give an inch. "I'll be fine, Mr.…."

"Abbot," he interrupted. "Marcus Abbot, but call me Marcus." He extended a hand.

Surprisingly she took it. Her grip was warm, but firm, and it struck him that he liked the way her small hand fit into his. And there was a hint of that heat again—more a slow burn than a jolt this time, but still bewitching.

She exhaled sharply and seemed to relax a tad. "I'm Dani Baxter."

He liked the name. It suited her. Confident, but a little quirky and sophisticated at the same time. And he noted there was no little gold band on her left hand.

"This is my daughter, Celeste, and her friend Katie." Dani touched the shoulder of each girl as she introduced them.

"We're here for a wedding," Celeste said excitedly. "It's our first time at the festival."

"Mine, too," Marcus said.

"Don't you just love it?" Katie asked.

"It's definitely looking up."

"Do you live around here?" Celeste asked.

"In Dobbin."

"I've never heard of it."

"It's a small town, just a few miles down the road."

"We live in Austin," Katie said. "You said you were in combat, but you look like a cowboy. So which one are you?"

"A former serviceman and a cowboy to the core."

"Do you have a ranch?" Celeste asked.

"No, but I live on one."

"With horses?"

"Lots of horses."

"Wow!"

"Yeah," Katie interjected. "I love horses."

He'd captured the girls' interest, but Dani was a harder sell. "You really should let me check your pulse again." This time when he reached for her wrist, she extended it.

"Back to normal," he said. Actually it was fast, barely noticeably so, but he decided to claim responsibility for the higher rate.

"See," she said, "just a harmless fainting spell, as I said. Nothing to worry about."

"Most likely," he agreed, "but I suggest you take it easy for a while. How about I buy you and the girls some lunch? Strictly as a medical professional looking after your health," he teased before "no" formed on her full, red lips.

"Thank you, but you've done more than enough."

"In that case, you should offer to buy mine," Marcus said, interrupting her protest with an argument he hoped she couldn't refuse.

A hint of a smile touched her mouth. She was weakening.

"Okay," she said. "Lunch it is. Choose your junk food booth."

Her color had returned, adding a healthy glow to her cheeks. She was damn good-looking. On a scale of one to ten, she might even top out at an eleven. But it was that episode back there where she looked as if she were dealing with the Devil that really had him going.

He'd bet a week's pay she was in some kind of trouble.

Dani strode away toward the nearest row of food stands. Back straight, head high, hips swaying. The view was every bit as good from the back as it had been from the front. Gorgeous and intriguing.

Yep. She needed him. She just didn't know it yet.

WITH FISH AND CHIPS and cold soft drinks in hand, Dani and Marcus settled at a wooden picnic table tucked under a tree next to a face-painting kiosk. The girls had taken their food and gone to catch the end of a juggling act a few yards away.

Marcus's presence flustered Dani. Partly, she decided, because he was too virile for comfort. But mostly because she was pretty sure he was about to hit her with questions she couldn't answer.

The fainting spell was a first for her. Even her worst psychic visions only stunned her, but all anyone ever noticed was that she lost her concentration.

Which meant this probably had nothing to do with her abilities. Perhaps she had spent too many hours out of town on business. She needed to slow down, and not let this green dress scenario ruin the whole festival experience.

"Great day for an outing," she said, going for a light tone that she didn't quite reach.

"The weather is definitely cooperating."

Marcus delved into his food as if he were starving. She picked at hers, her usually hearty appetite nonexistent. She was *almost* convinced the episode in the shop hadn't been a trance with deeper meaning, so why couldn't she shake it from her mind?

"You're not eating," Marcus said. "Don't you like the fish?"

"I do. It's a bit salty, but the flavor is good."

"But you have something else on your mind?"

He was much too perceptive. "I was just thinking of my friend's wedding," she lied.

"Do you disapprove of it?"

"Not exactly. I've never met the groom, but the bride has two failed marriages on her resume. I know I'd be scared to death to go for a third."

"All marriages scare me."

"Does that mean you're single?"

"I am now. My first attempt crashed and burned."

"Ah, that explains the fear of commitment."

"Let's just say I know enough to avoid playing catch with a hand grenade. What about you? I don't see a wedding band."

"I'm divorced."

"Stupid man."

"Thanks. He wouldn't agree. He likes to trade up."

"Oh, one of those gotta-have-this-year's-model type."

"You got it. And you?"

He grinned. "My pickup truck is practically an antique."

Dani took a bite of the fish. Crispy crumbs of

coating sprinkled her blouse. She brushed them away with her napkin. Marcus used his to dab at a tidbit that must have stuck to her chin.

His hand lingered a moment too long, and a tingle of awareness shot through her. Not psychic but pure sensual attraction. To her credit, she knew the difference. Well, most of the time she knew the difference.

She poked a fry into her mouth and nibbled while she put things in perspective. Even if she were receiving genuine psychic messages—which she didn't believe—there really was nothing she could do about it. She couldn't identify anyone involved. Case closed.

She might as well enjoy the moment. The fascinating cowboy whose smile and easy mannerisms promised any manner of sexual pleasures would be out of her life in a matter of minutes.

That was fine, too. As nice as it might be to sample his virility, she simply didn't have time to add the complications of a long-distance relationship with no chance of succeeding to her extremely busy life.

She finished her meal with a lot more enthusiasm than she'd begun it. Once she'd wiped the grease from her mouth and hands, she wadded the napkin and started to get up.

Marcus reached out and wrapped his hand around her arm.

Her breath caught on the intake. "My pulse is fine," she said, though she was pretty sure it was racing. No way she could deny such a dynamic attraction. "And I really do need to get back to the girls. We'll have to pick up the pace if we want to cover the festival before sundown."

"About the fainting spell…"

She shook her head, feeling more confident now that she'd thought the incident through. "Not going there again, cowboy."

"Fair enough, but take this." He pulled a

business card from his pocket and pressed it into her hand. “Call me anytime. I’ll come running.”

“What, running and not riding up on a white steed? Where’s your festival spirit?”

“The steed can be arranged.”

“It sounds incredibly tempting,” she admitted, “but we’re only here until tomorrow afternoon, and the wedding activities will take most of our time.” She slipped the card in her pocket without looking at it.

“If I can help with anything, don’t hesitate to call.”

“I won’t.” Nor could she imagine a situation in which she’d need the services of a cowboy. Well, there was one, but that involved the romantic entanglement that she had zero time for. She started to gather the trash.

“I’ll take care of it,” he said. “Go enjoy the festival, but don’t lose that card.” He stood and then in a suavely, smooth move touched his lips to hers.

Heat shot through her in waves, and it was all she could do not to melt into his arms. Fortunately, his lips didn't remain on hers long enough to give her the chance. She walked away while she still could, much too aware of the card and phone number that lay buried in the pocket of her new designer jeans.

Once she'd put a few yards between them, she glanced back and found Marcus still standing in the exact same spot as she'd left him. Their eyes locked, and he smiled and tipped his hat. Her heart flipped in response.

"Dani!"

The squeal jolted her out of her momentary sensual relapse. To her rear might be a gorgeous cowboy, but in front of her was Bethany Sue. Not the same Bethany Sue she remembered, however.

The pudgy ally she'd known for years was absolutely svelte now. And radiant. She positively glowed.

The two collided in a genuine hug. "You look great," Dani said when they separated from each other and stepped back.

"Thanks." Bethany Sue did a catwalk turn for her to get the full effect. "I owe it all to Arnie. He persuaded me to quit smoking, start working out and to eat healthy."

Dani was sure she owed part of the new her to a plastic surgeon, but she let that ride. More power to her for taking control of her body and her life.

"I can't wait to meet the lucky groom."

"You'll love him. He's a body builder and personal trainer. A real hunk! But not all muscle. He's got brains, too."

"He sounds fascinating."

"He is. And he's dying to meet you. I've told him all about you, my friend. The winner of the state math competition and karaoke queen."

"Oh, God, that was so long ago. Can we just go with mother and buyer for Duran Muton?"

"You look far more like a model than a buyer. But speaking of motherhood, where is Celeste? She did come, didn't she?"

"She and a friend. They're over there, absorbed in a juggling act." Dani nodded toward the crowd seated on concrete benches shaded by a web of net and intertwined branches.

"Great. I'll catch up with both of you at the dinner tonight. I'm rushing off right now to reconfirm the setup for the tables and to make sure they have plenty of champagne. Everything will be outdoors."

"Perfect weather for that. Is there anything I can do to help?"

"No, just enjoy yourself, unless…" She hesitated.

"This doesn't have anything to do with the guy you wanted me to meet, does it?"

"No," Bethany assured her. "But you'll probably be begging me to fix you up once you see him."

"Don't count on it. So, how can I help?"

"Arnie's sister is supposed to sing at the ceremony, but she woke up this morning with a terrible headache and a fever. She thinks she may be coming down with the flu."

The one thing worse than a blind date. "I haven't sung in front of an audience in years."

"You're kidding, right?"

"No, and it's not that shocking, Bethany. I was never that good."

"Yes, you were. If there had been an *American Idol* back then, you'd have won in a landslide." Bethany glanced at her watch. "I have to go, but consider singing for me at the ceremony, please. It's just two songs. We'll talk more tonight. Gotta run." She gave Dani a parting hug.

"I'm seriously out of practice," Dani called after her.

Bethany either didn't hear or chose to ignore her. Dani imagined it was the latter. She'd protest again tonight, but it would be a wasted effort. Bethany was not one to take no for a final answer, and it would be pretty crummy to refuse a bride in distress.

The good thing was that other than Celeste and Katie, she would neither know the guests nor have to face them again after she murdered the music.

Murdered. Even thinking the word gave her chills after this morning's hallucinations. They'd been so intense that Dani had actually felt the thrust of the blade as it punctured the walls of the chest and sliced into the victim's heart—as if it were happening to her.

In broad daylight. Eyes wide open, at least they had been until she'd passed out.

"You should have seen the jugglers, Mom. They were funny and really good."

Startled, Dani jumped and then spun around to face the girls.

"Are you okay?" Katie asked. "You look kind of pale."

"Eeks, you do," Celeste agreed. "You're not going to faint again, are you?"

"I'm not pale. I just haven't gotten enough sun lately. Today's the day for it."

"Where'd the cute cowboy go?" Katie asked.

"Who needs a cute cowboy when I have you two? Now tell me about the jugglers." She forced the disturbing memories to the back of her mind. She had to get a hold of her emotions and regain her stability before she turned this whole weekend into a fiasco.

"The jugglers were really cool," Katie said, thankfully changing the topic of conversation. "They even juggled fiery batons."

"And they threw a knife and chopped the end off a carrot a woman was holding in her mouth." Celeste used her hand to show how close the knife had come to the woman's nose. "I never would have trusted them to try that with me."

"Good for you," Dani said. "Any ideas what

we should do next, or should we just walk and take in the sights?"

"A boy sitting next to us said we should be sure and go to the jousting exhibition," Katie said. "He said it's all staged but that it looks real and sometimes the guys get knocked off their horses."

"And you can cheer for whichever rider you want to win," Celeste added, then turned to watch a rickshaw go by that was being pulled by a scantily clad slave lad. The pseudo lord and lady riding in the cart waved.

"This is so neat," Katie said. "Like taking a time machine into the past. I can't wait until we get our costumes for tonight's party."

Dani wasn't quite up to that yet. She checked the program and her watch. "The next jousting exhibition is at one o'clock. That gives us twenty minutes, if you want to make that performance."

"Let's do it," Celeste and Katie said in unison.

A few seconds later they'd checked the map

and were on their way across the festival grounds to the day's next adventure. The girls hurried ahead but stopped frequently to peek at wares on display outside of the shops—jewelry; sandals; pewter, fire-breathing dragons cast in stone. Some findings were far more authentic than others. All of them captured the Renaissance spirit.

The spirit of revelry started to dissolve Dani's misgivings about having come here today. Maybe the warning was just for her not to buy a green dress for the party or wedding. No problem there. She'd go in her jeans first.

But suppose someone else wore that dress to the party, maybe even Bethany Sue?

She shook her head to clear it, then stood perfectly still when she got this disconcerting feeling that someone was watching her. She turned. No one was paying her the slightest attention, not with two busty wenches posing for pictures near the beer stand.

If she was going to be this jumpy all weekend, she should just pack it up and go home. Or perhaps she should have held on to the sexy cowboy a while longer, even invited him to the party tonight as her guest. A new image took hold in her mind, this one of her in Marcus Abbot's arms, dancing beneath a star-studded sky.

The slow burn that settled between her thighs sent a quick flush to her cheeks. Lusting after strangers was not her style. She had to get out more. It had been months—no, make that a solid year—since she'd had any intimate contact with a man.

With good reason, she reminded herself. Her last date had been a miserable exercise in how much boredom she could endure.

As a group of sexy wenches passed, a young teenage boy walked up to her and stuck out a note. "I'm supposed to give you this."

Dani took the slip of paper and read the message that was printed in black ink.

Beware of the dark knight.

The boy started to walk away. She slipped the note into her pocket and hurried to catch up with him. "Why did you give me that?"

"That man back there asked me to."

"What man? Show me."

He looked around. "I don't see him now, but he was standing right back there by that tree a minute ago."

"Was he wearing a cowboy hat?"

"Naw."

"In costume?"

The kid shook his head. "He was just dressed like a regular dude. Had on a blue polo shirt. That's all I know."

A blue knit shirt, like the man she'd thought was watching her in the dress shop. "Did he have dark brown hair?"

"Yeah, maybe. I gotta go catch up with my friends."

Dani pulled out the note and reread it, growing more perturbed by the second. She stuffed it back into her pocket when she saw the girls approaching.

"Hey, Mom, you dropped this."

The cowboy's business card. Dani must have lost it when she was fiddling with the note.

"Marcus Abbot," Celeste read from the card. "Double M Investigation and Protection Service. No boundaries, No limits. No job too tough." She handed the card back to Dani.

"Cool. A Rambo," Katie said.

"I think that means he's a private detective, not a commando," Dani said. But the card did advertise protection and no limits. She could hire him. And he'd laugh her right off the planet when she told him she needed protection from a dark knight.

"There's the jousting arena," Katie said, pointing dead ahead of them to a huge circular wall adorned by busts.

Beware the dark knight.

A dagger plunged into a woman's heart.

"Hurry, Mom. We want to get a good seat."

Marcus's card felt as if it were burning the palm of her hand, all but making the decision for her. "Go ahead," she called. "Save me a seat. Something's come up at work, and I have to make a quick phone call."

She might have a date for tonight's party after all.

Chapter Three

Marcus was watching a pair of youngsters being hoisted onto the back of a large and extremely wrinkled elephant when his cell phone rang. The caller ID merely indicated a wireless connection. He punched the talk button. “Hello?”

“Marcus?”

He recognized the voice at once. “At your service.”

“This is Dani Baxter. We had lunch together a few minutes ago.”

A reminder, as if she were that easy to forget. "Glad you called. What's up?"

Too many seconds of silence followed. "Are you okay, Dani?"

"Yeah. I'm fine. No more fainting," she added hurriedly.

"Good." She sounded rattled.

"I was just looking at your card, and I have what may sound like a strange request."

"Strange is my specialty."

"I'd like you to be my guest tonight for the prewedding party. It's on the festival grounds at eight o'clock."

Not what he was expecting.

"I'll pay you, of course," Dani added, as he tried to figure out what was going on here.

"You must be looking at the wrong card. The Double M is not an escort service."

"I realize that. I'm not looking for an escort. I think—I mean it's possible—I mean... Look, I'll explain it all later, but the truth is

I'll feel better if I know the girls and I are in your hands tonight."

That was more like it. "Are you in danger, Dani?"

"I'm not sure. Probably not. It's just that..."

The woman was a wreck, and she hadn't seemed the irrational type. "Are you sure you're okay? I'm right here on the grounds. I could probably catch up with you in minutes."

"No. Look, I really can't talk now, but I'll explain everything tonight."

Somehow he doubted that. But even if she continued to skirt the issue, he'd get the truth out of her eventually. That actually was one of his specialties. Women trusted him. He used to trust them. "When and where do I pick you up?"

"We're staying at a bed-and-breakfast in Magnolia, but you can just meet us here."

"I'm old-fashioned. I like to pick up my date at her door."

"This isn't really a date."

"Humor me. Besides, I work better with a full lay of the land."

"I don't want the girls to know I've hired you. I was thinking we could just make it look as if we hooked up at the party."

So he was to be a secret date. A warning bell sounded. More often than not when a woman was running scared, a husband or lover was involved. "Does this situation have to do with your significant other?"

"No, of course not. I wouldn't be hooking up, pretend or otherwise, if I had a significant other."

"It's been done."

"Not by me. I'm divorced and have been for years."

And that was probably all he'd get out of her until tonight. "According to the schedule, the festival is not open at night, so how do I get in to this party?"

"Invitation only." She sighed. "You'll have to attend as my guest, so maybe it would be best if you pick me up at the B and B. I'll think of some way to explain all this to Celeste and Katie, but I definitely don't want them to know that I'm hiring you."

Not surprising since she hadn't even told him the why as yet. "How about I pick you up at seven-thirty?"

"That would work. The invitation encourages guests to come in the style of the Elizabethan period."

"There I draw the line. I don't do costumes."

"Frankly, at this point, I'm not sure I do, either."

She gave him the name of the B and B she'd booked and the directions she'd gotten on the Internet. Then she said a quick goodbye and broke their connection before he could ask more questions.

Too bad, since dozens stalked his mind. He figured there was at least a ninety-nine percent chance his being hired as a protector was connected to the fainting spell she'd experienced that morning. Judging from the look in her eyes at the time, he'd have sworn she was wrestling demons.

But what or who had her spooked? A stalker? An ex-lover? Someone in costume that she might not recognize until it was too late? That could present a few problems.

Nothing he couldn't handle. He wouldn't take his eyes off her for a second. That part would be easy.

Remembering this was a job and not a date with a beautiful, sophisticated woman might take a bit more skill.

A ROAR ROSE from the crowd as Dani entered the amphitheater. The tiers of concrete benches surrounded a dirt performance area that four partially armored knights circled on magnificent steeds. Behind them a viewing stand filled with exquisitely dressed lords and ladies.

Cheers and jeers rose from the crowd as each knight and his cheerleader lady tried to drum up support for their quest.

She glanced around, looking for the girls. The sea of faces became a blur.

"Over here, Ms. Baxter." Katie's high-pitched voice barely carried over the din. "We saved you a seat."

The twelve-year-old with her wild mass of red hair only partially tamed by a baseball cap was sitting on the end of a bench just a few rows up from where Dani was standing. Alone.

Unexpected anxiety rolled in Dani's stomach. "Where's Celeste?"

"Buying cotton candy." Katie pointed to their left where Celeste was counting out bills to a vendor whose colorful bags of sugary sweets floated above him like balloons, each secured to his long pole.

Safe, of course. This was a family festival meant to lift the spirits, not some Halloweenish house of ancient horrors. Dani was freaking out over nothing and everything. And now she'd hired a bodyguard who'd surely think she was a certifiable nutcase.

Dani slid to the seat beside Katie. "What did I miss?"

"The introduction of the knights. We're rooting for the one representing France. He has the best horse and the prettiest lady leading the cheers for him. But the rider from Spain has our school colors, so we're kinda for him, too."

Celeste rejoined them and held out the cone of blue twirled sugar for them to share. "You got here just in time, Mom. I was afraid you were going to miss the jousting. You already missed a lot of the fun."

"I'm here now. Let the games begin." Dani forced a carefree cheerfulness into her voice and tore off a bite-size piece of the froth. Her irritation with herself swelled.

For once Celeste was truly enjoying their day together, and Dani was the one putting a damper on the excitement.

The crowd began to cheer as the four knights returned. Each wore an armored chest piece. Jointed armor covered parts of their arms and legs as well.

The horses were draped in the same vibrant hues as their riders' flowing tunics. One was dressed in black and silver and had a sinister air about him. The jovial air of pageantry and the crowd's fervent reactions were truly impressive.

The knights circled the arena on the horses, waving to the spectators and pumping up the enthusiasm. One, a young blonde with a disarming smile, tended to steal the show.

"That's the contender from France," Celeste said when he waved in their direction.

Dani was sure the show was scripted, the winners and losers predetermined on a rotational basis, but that took little from the performance's exuberance. The excitement arced even higher as the announcer proclaimed that the tournament was to begin.

Each of the riders pulled on helmets that looked official but still somewhat like silver pots. They waved their long, striped poles in the air as if they couldn't wait to attack. Two riders came at each other from opposite corners, ferociously striking out with their poles as they met at midfield. As soon as they'd reached their corners, the other two followed suit.

Celeste and Katie stayed fully engrossed for the duration of the engagement. Dani quickly drifted back into her own thoughts and was relieved when only one contender remained on his horse, the jouster clad in black and silver. He was declared the winner amidst more yells and some heckling and then was toasted by the approving lords and ladies in the viewing stand.

With so many open arches providing exits, the arena cleared quickly. Dani and the girls lingered for a few minutes so that they could get an up-close look at one of the knights who'd stayed around to talk to a group of admiring females.

By the time they left, there were only a few other stragglers ambling through the wide center arch. They took the path that led toward the giant swings. There seemed to be more people than ever milling around the area.

An auburn-haired woman in an exquisite period ball gown pushed past them, practically knocking Dani down in her haste. She paused as if to apologize but said nothing. Instead, she stared at Dani, a look of alarm on her face.

Their eyes met, and Dani had a crushing sensation of déjà vu. "Have we met before?"

"No," the woman answered quickly. She hurried away before Dani could say more.

"Geez," Katie said. "That woman looks almost like you, Ms. Baxter."

"Except she's not as pretty," Celeste said. "She's too skinny, and her hair's the wrong color."

"You weren't even looking at her!" Katie exclaimed. "You were watching those guys at the climbing wall. And she did so look like your mother."

"I have that generic look," Dani said, dismissing the comparison. "People are always saying someone looks like me."

That wasn't exactly true, and Dani had noticed a remarkable similarity between her and the woman. But it was the feeling that she knew her or had at least met her before that had really captured Dani's attention.

Could she possibly be the woman from the nightmare?

The hair was close enough. The eyes could be the same color. She wasn't sure about anything else. There hadn't been time to get a good look at her before the woman had hurried away.

And here she was falling back into the green dress trap. Coming to this wedding had definitely been a mistake. At this rate, she was going to have a nervous breakdown before they got back to Austin.

"Let's go get our outfits for the party and wedding now," Celeste said. "I can't wait to pick mine out."

Next the costumes, then the dinner party with the ruggedly handsome cowboy along for the ride. She may as well enjoy that part, though he'd no doubt think her totally mad when she explained why she'd hired him.

She was beginning to think the same thing herself.

ELLA SOMERVILLE'S headache approached migraine status as she hurried away from the woman who looked much too much like her for comfort. It was the second time today they'd crossed paths. The first time had been this morning when the woman had fainted in the festival dress shop that Ella managed. The woman hadn't seen her, but Ella had been there.

Fortunately, that was over quickly enough when the man in the black hat came to her rescue. Running into her the second time was even more unsettling. It was an omen, the push she needed to leave the Renaissance circuit for good.

The danger lay in getting comfortable in a routine. Predictability created risk. Even if she had to just give the trailer to Kevin, it was time to go. Things weren't working out between them anyway, especially now that his buddy Billy Germaine had joined the jousting team.

She'd come back to the travel trailer for pain-killers for the pounding in her temples, but she might just stay here now and rest for a while. She needed to get rid of the headache since she was signed on to work tonight as a server for an after-hours shindig.

Even that didn't seem such a good idea now, but she could use the extra cash.

She pulled her keys from her pocket, then came to a quick halt when she heard Kevin's and Billy's voices coming from inside the trailer. Kevin sounded angry. That didn't surprise her. She'd warned him not to get in so deep with Billy.

The guy was trouble. He reeked of it. Not to mention that he'd hit on her a few days after joining the troupe, when he knew good and well she and Kev were a couple. Not that they were married or ever would be, but they were living together.

Billy was dating a lady who worked in one of the jewelry shops now. Connie Rincon. She loved jewelry, especially if it included dragons in its design. A nice lady, way too good for Billy.

Ella tugged the floppy, feathered hat from her head with her right hand and fit the key into the lock. The door opened a few inches before she turned it. Kevin never bothered to lock it.

Billy spit out a stream of curses. Ella hesitated, listening as the conversation grew more heated. The accusations made her stomach roll. This had to be some kind of sick joke.

But, no, Kevin was growing angrier by the second. The key slipped from her shaking fingers and clattered to the threshold. The talk stopped immediately.

"Is that you, Ella?"

"It's me, Kev. I have a headache. I didn't have any meds with me so I came back to the trailer to get some."

"How long have you been standing there?" Billy demanded.

"I just walked up." Her voice faltered on the lie. She tossed her hat to an empty chair so that she could look away and avoid eye contact.

"Did you get an ear full?"

"Leave her alone," Kev said. "She already has a headache."

Billy crushed his empty beer can. "Women who talk too much wind up in the morgue, Ella. That's a fact of life. Did you ever hear that saying before?"

"Sounds like beer talking to me," she said. "You guys go ahead and visit. I'm just going to pop some pills and go back to the shop."

"Why not take off if you're sick?" Kev asked. "You're the boss."

"That's why I can't," she said, looking for any excuse to get away from him and Billy. "There's a party on the grounds tonight and four weddings tomorrow. People will need outfits for those and that translates to a busy afternoon. And don't forget that I'm doing table duty tonight for the caterer, so I won't be home until after that."

"Try not to be too late," he said. There was

no hint that he suspected she'd overheard the damning conversation.

Still, it was time to move on.

DANI FELT LIKE Queen Guinevere waiting for Sir Lancelot to ride up on a white horse and steal her away as she stared into the full-length mirror. Her dress was exquisite and just a tad daring.

The girls had picked it out, though it hadn't been their first choice. That one had been green, not anything like the gown in her nightmarish illusions, but green nonetheless. She'd vetoed it immediately.

This one was sapphire-blue, in a fabric that shimmered and picked up the light like a million dancing jewels. Her inherited, cherished pearl amulet on its golden chain added the perfect finishing touch. Grams had always claimed it had mystical powers that could save the one wearing it from any number of evil deeds.

Dani had yet to put it to the test. She planned to keep it that way.

"Wow, Ms. Baxter, you look super," Katie exclaimed as she slipped through the door that separated their adjoining rooms.

"Thank you, Katie. I feel super."

"Good. Celeste and I were afraid you were coming down with the flu or something when you passed out this morning."

The flu would have been a much more credible excuse than low blood sugar, especially when Celeste knew her eating habits so well. But who could think when they'd just snapped out of a mind-numbing trance to find themselves staring into the whiskey-colored eyes of a gorgeous cowboy? The same cowboy who would show up at their door any minute now.

Dani turned her focus to Katie and her multicolored skirt topped by an embroidery-trimmed pale pink peasant blouse. "You make an adorable lady-in-waiting. I don't think I've ever seen you with your hair up."

"Celeste did the upsweep for me. Do you like it?"

No. Having the wild mass of red curls tied at the top of her head made the almost-teen look much too old and far more sophisticated than she was. Nonetheless…

"You look enchanting," she said truthfully.

"Hey, Mom, I need help with this zipper. It's stuck."

Celeste burst through the door, the hem of her skirt pulled to her waist. Her shiny brown hair fell in straight but silky strands halfway down her back. Her attire was the same as Katie's except her blouson was deep purple and fell over flat breasts instead of Katie's developing ones.

Still my little girl, but not for long, Dani thought as she took over the task of freeing the metal zipper teeth from the gauzy fabric.

"Coming here is the neatest thing we've done in like forever," Celeste said as the zipper pulled free and the skirt fell to her ankles. "I can't wait to see what the entertainment is like tonight. I bet those jugglers will be part of it."

"Yeah, they were good. I want to get my picture with them so I can show the girls at school. I bet nobody in our class has ever been to a Renaissance wedding."

"Right, not even snobby Samantha Cotter, and she's been everywhere."

"But her mother is not nearly as pretty as you are, Ms. Baxter. She'd never score a date with a hot cowboy she'd just met like you did."

"I told you it's not a date," Dani stressed. "Marcus was going to the party anyway, and he just offered to escort us so that we wouldn't have to drive back alone tonight on those dark, narrow roads."

"No, he's hot for you," Celeste said. "I could tell. He knows you're fun."

Fun? Dani felt like she'd been anything but lately. That had to change. She needed this weekend to go well, for her sake and Celeste's. She touched the amulet at her neck and thought of Marcus and his teasing smile.

The tenseness started to ease, and her customary confidence picked up steam. They were here to celebrate with Bethany Sue, and it was foolish to keep worrying about things she could do nothing about.

A knock at the door captured all their attention. Celeste swung it open, and there stood Marcus, dressed in hip-hugging jeans, boots and his black Stetson—and looking even sexier than he had been this morning. Who'd have thought that was possible?

Their eyes met, and the temperature in the room seemed to jump a few dozen degrees. Not a date. This time she reminded herself of that fact. It did nothing to still the heated anticipation that was fast turning her insides to molten gold.

Chapter Four

Marcus struggled to keep his eyes focused straight ahead and his mind and body from drowning in unadulterated lust as he drove the meandering blacktop roads to the festival grounds. If it weren't for the two youthful chaperones in the backseat, he might have sneaked an arm around Dani's beautiful shoulders and let his thumb ride the stately column of her neck.

Talk about totally inappropriate behavior for a man being paid to protect.

He was beginning to wonder if some other

far more trusting guy had crawled into his skin. Not that he wasn't as susceptible as the next male when it came to getting turned on by a shapely body and a pretty face. He'd been attracted to Dani from the moment she'd sashayed by him and into the dress shop this morning. He just didn't usually let his urges get as out of control as they were right now.

But Dani Baxter, with her sultry, Southern charm and striking Elizabethan gown, defied the odds. She had an almost mystical quality about her tonight. The effect was magnified a thousand times when she touched her long, manicured fingers to the delicate charm resting just above the swell of her breasts and their intoxicating cleavage.

He forced his concentration back to the road and tightened his grip on the steering wheel, determined to rein in his libido. If he wasn't careful, he'd lose the instincts he'd developed as a cowboy and refined to the nth degree as a frogman.

The cowboy elements of his personality kept him sane. The SEAL qualities kept him on the fighting edge, aware of every nuance of change in his environment and the people around him.

In spite of Dani's attempts at lightheartedness since he'd picked her up, he knew she was still dealing with the same demons he'd seen reflected in the deep cinnamon pools of her eyes this morning.

Unfortunately, merely knowing that was not enough information for him to do his job well. He planned to get a lot more facts out of her the second they were out of the girls' earshot.

For one thing, he didn't see Dani Baxter as the swoon-and-faint type. She seemed a lot more like a take-charge filly. Self-assured. Spunky. But something had definitely spooked her today.

By the time they reached the festival grounds, he was firmly back in his operational frogman mode, detached from emotion and ready for anything the night threw at him.

That lasted until they reached the gate, and she linked her arm with his, just as a muscle-bound king and voluptuous queen rushed toward them.

"The bride and I'm guessing the groom," Dani murmured, and then let go of his arm to plunge into a bear hug with the queen.

They exchanged introductions all around. He liked Bethany Sue instantly. She had a naive, girlish quality about her that made her enthusiasm seem genuine.

The groom was still up for debate. His muscles knotted all the way up to his thick neck, but strength did not always equate with toughness. Marcus knew that well from his stint with the SEALs. Some of the bravest, hard-hitting frogmen he'd known were half Arnie's size.

"I thought you said you weren't bringing a

date," Bethany Sue said. "And then you show up with this hunky cowboy."

"Change of plans at the last minute," Dani replied, trying to brush off the interest. "And you said the more the merrier."

"Absolutely. You look stunning, girlfriend. That gown is to die for."

"I owe full credit to Celeste and Katie. They picked it out."

"Ohmigod," Bethany said, as if she'd just spied the girls. "You two look like confections in a candy shop. Love those shimmering skirts."

"This is such a cool idea for a wedding," Celeste said.

"Yeah," Katie agreed. "Way better than just walking down a plain old church aisle."

"The ceremony will be in a wedding chapel," Bethany Sue said. "There are several of them right here on the grounds."

"Wow. Perfect," Katie said.

"This was all Arnie's idea," Bethany explained. "He has friends who travel the Renaissance circuit a few months out of every year. You'll meet them later tonight. They operate a couple of concessions at the festival—one who sells antique-style jewelry and one who deals in knives and swords."

Marcus listened to the rest of the conversation, hoping for verbal clues as to what had led to Dani's hiring him for the evening. He probably came across as less than attentive, but he was absorbing a dozen things at once.

The chatter. The setup for tonight's dinner and entertainment. The lighting. The location of security cameras. Pockets of darkness. Basically, he wanted a blueprint in his mind of any and everything that would affect his providing protection for Dani and the girls.

When Arnie and Bethany Sue moved on to a group of new arrivals, he maneuvered Dani and the girls toward a face-painting booth set up near the tables and chairs circling a portable dance floor.

"Did I hear someone in the backseat of the truck on the way over say they wanted body art to complete their costume?"

The girls jumped and squealed their agreement. Who knew teenage girls squealed so much?

Once they'd chosen their designs, Marcus tugged Dani aside. "I'd be able to do my job a lot better if I had some facts."

The expression on her face changed to one of pure dread. He put a hand to her shoulder and then pulled it away too quickly. Just touching her had some kind of bewitching effect on him, and he needed his head clear for this.

Dani fingered the pendant. "What if I said I just called you because I wanted to see you again?"

"I'd be damned flattered and a sight more gullible than I am if I believed you."

She nodded, a look of resolution finally

settling in her haunted eyes. "Okay, and if you charge me double for wasting your time, I'll fully understand."

DANI HAD DELIBERATED all afternoon on exactly how much she should confess to Marcus. She'd told no one in her adult life that her grandmother was clairvoyant. The only person she still had any contact with who knew about her inherited curse was Bethany Sue, and she had been sworn to secrecy years ago.

Under no circumstances did she ever intend for her daughter to find out about her psychic gifts—which was why she couldn't even consider telling Marcus the whole truth. If she breathed a word of her fears that this morning's episode might possibly have been a psychic vision, it would let her paranormal skeletons out of the closet to rattle their bones around Celeste.

Plus, he'd dismiss her as a kook.

That left Dani only one realistic alternative. She pulled the note from her pocket, smoothed it with her fingertips and handed it to him.

"Someone at the festival gave me this. It's probably nothing, but it frightened me when I read it. That's when I decided to call you."

He grimaced as he studied the note. "Did you see the person who delivered it?"

"Yes. It was a young teenage boy, but he was just the messenger. All he could tell me about the man who gave it to him was that he was wearing a blue polo shirt."

"That's it?"

"Yes, but when I was shopping earlier today, I noticed a man in a blue knit shirt staring at me. Well, I didn't exactly see him, but I saw his reflection in the mirror. When I turned to see if I knew him, he ducked out of sight. It might not have even been the same man, but I found the possibility a bit disturbing. Hence my call to you."

"Do you have any idea who the dark knight refers to?"

"Not even a clue. The only people I know here besides you and the girls are Bethany Sue and Arnie, and I only just met him." For that matter she'd just met Marcus, as well.

"There are no shortage of knight wannabes milling around us tonight," Marcus noted.

"It was probably from someone just getting into the spirit of the festival," she said.

"Or hitting on you, though sending a note like this is an odd way to score points."

"I'm thinking it could have been a case of mistaken identity. There is someone else at the festival today who looks a lot like me. The two of us practically collided when I was leaving the jousting arena."

"Is this the first threat or warning of this nature you've received?"

"Absolutely."

"And the first time you've noticed that man was this morning?"

"Yes. And that was before I fainted, so that can't be why he was staring at me—if he *was* actually staring at me."

"I know you said you're not seriously involved with anyone, but what about your nonserious love life?"

"That's pretty much a draw between Brad Pitt, Hugh Jackman and George Clooney. As yet, they haven't participated."

"No stalkers?"

"Not since college."

"What about someone you may have dumped who didn't take it well?"

"I haven't been in any serious relationships since my ex."

"And he's totally out of your life now?"

"Except for a few guest appearances as Celeste's father, and he avoids those unless it suits him."

"Then you don't know of anyone who'd have reason to harm you?"

"No." Which made her hiring him sound all the more ridiculous. "I probably overreacted," she admitted. "I should never have called you."

He nudged his Stetson a little lower on his forehead and leveled his gaze at her. "What really happened this morning in that costume shop, Dani?"

A cold knot settled just below her breastbone. This was the exact path she didn't want the conversation to take.

"I've been under a lot of stress at work." Not a total lie. "I guess it took its toll."

He looked skeptical. "I'm here on your dollar, Dani, so you can stick with any story you want. But you clearly had more going on than mental fatigue when the salesperson held that green dress in front of you."

She looked away. "I don't know what you're talking about."

"I'm talking about your need to level with

me. You're running scared. I think there's more to that than someone handing you a note."

She sucked in a huge gulp of the bracing fall air. It was as if the man could see right through her. Obviously, he couldn't or he'd be running in the opposite direction.

A small band began to play in the background. People were starting to take their seats in anticipation of the predinner entertainment.

"You can trust me, Dani."

Marcus's words wrapped around her. She met his gaze again and sank into the depths of his eyes. It was tempting to take him at his word. So very tempting.

"You'll think I'm nuts."

"Try me."

He stepped closer, reached over and took her hand in his. The warmth of his touch added a new layer of vulnerability to her senses.

She had to be very, very careful what she said at this point. "I had a nightmare about a month ago," she admitted reluctantly. "It was incredibly vivid and disturbing, and I haven't been able to totally shake it from my mind."

"What happened in this nightmare?"

"A woman was murdered while wearing an Elizabethan ball gown very similar to the one I was looking at when I fainted." She hesitated. Even to her the explanation sounded bizarre. She'd already said too much. "Believe me, I'm as baffled by this as you are, but apparently the whole thing just got to me."

"Was the woman in the dream someone you knew?"

"Not really, except that…" Dani shuddered.

Marcus stepped closer and reached for her hand. "Go on."

Her breath caught, and she did a hard intake of oxygen. "You know how nightmares are. I thought the woman might be me, but I didn't actually see her face."

He squeezed her hand. "No wonder seeing

the dress and then getting the note made you nervous."

"I still feel foolish for letting the situation get out of hand over a nightmare. I'm sorry for wasting your time tonight, and if you want to leave right now, I'll not only understand but still pay the full amount I owe you."

"And miss the party?" He flashed his devastating smile. "Besides, a deal's a deal, and it's not often I get to spend the evening in old England with a beautiful woman."

Moonlight, music and the company of Marcus Abbot. If she could put the whole premonition of danger behind her, it just might be the best deal she'd struck in years.

THE REST OF THE EVENING passed without even a glimmer of trouble, unless you counted Marcus's total infatuation with Dani Baxter a problem. She got to him on a number of levels, not the least of which was that he hadn't totally bought her story of why she'd come to him for protection.

The more he talked to her the more he realized just how levelheaded she was. It was obvious she was a great mother, and she had a responsible job that she was apparently good at.

All said, it made it difficult to imagine that she'd let a nightmare cause the kind of reaction he'd witnessed this morning. It had been more than just passing out. She'd been two-stepping with terror—at least it had looked that way to him.

"You two should dance," Celeste encouraged.

"I have two left feet, big left feet," he said, sticking out one of his booted feet to prove his point. "Stomp on dainty toes with these clod-hoppers and it could break bones."

Actually he wasn't that bad of a dancer when they were playing a boot-scootin' number, but the tune the band was dishing out now sounded like a cross between a minuet and a watered-down Hail to the Queen. Still, there were several couples on the floor including the bride and groom.

Dani eyed his feet. "Those are big enough that I should be able to stay out of the way of them."

An invitation from her own gorgeous mouth to take her in his arms. What sane man could turn that down? He stood and put out a hand. Hers fit into his like warm velvet.

Just as they reached a clear spot for him to make his missteps, the song ended and a new one began. This time it was one of those slow, belly-rubbing numbers that made a man have bedroom thoughts. The dance floor filled up quickly.

He splayed his fingers across her back and pulled her close. Her body melded against his, and the nearness made it impossible for him to do more than sway to the sensual beat. Finally his equilibrium returned enough that he could move his feet.

She even smelled good. Admittedly, he had

years of being around nothing but sweaty guys in fatigues, so it didn't take all that much to titillate his senses. At any rate, his senses were reeling now.

She rested her head on his shoulder as their bodies moved with the music. He'd missed holding a woman more than he'd ever want to admit. He'd never been unfaithful once in his years in the military. He'd thought marriage meant fidelity. And then he'd come home to find he was the only one living in that dream world.

The song ended much too soon.

"Do you have any broken bones?" Celeste teased as they rejoined the girls at the table.

"*Au contraire.* Marcus is a very good dancer."

"I had a good partner," Marcus said. He held Dani's chair while she slid her adorable behind into it and rearranged her skirt. His gaze slid to the cleavage peeking above the neckline of her blouse. Heat rushed through him like a California forest fire, and he backed away quickly before his body became noticeably hard.

It was a damn good thing she was going back to Austin tomorrow. As much as he liked being with her, he didn't want things to get out of hand. He had plans for his life. They didn't include falling in love and giving a beautiful, successful woman a chance to stamp his heart back into the ground.

Besides, she was a client. A bodyguard worth his salt never fell for the person he was being paid to protect. Lust, yes. Emotional entanglement, never.

He reached for a piece of bread from the basket that had been set in the middle of the table while they'd danced. "Looks like food is on the way," he said.

"Yeah, and remember that woman we saw this afternoon," Katie said, "the one who looks like you, Ms. Baxter?"

"What about her?" Dani asked, her voice suddenly strained.

"She's one of the waitresses here tonight."

"Is she our waitress?" Marcus asked.

"She didn't bring our bread, but she was carrying trays of water around. She's in costume, too. I think we should get a picture of the two of you together, Ms. Baxter."

Dani shifted in her seat and crossed her arms in front of her. "Can we just forget about that woman?"

"Sure," Celeste agreed. "But it would make a good picture, and I bet she wouldn't mind."

"How about pointing her out to me when you see her again?" Marcus said. He reached for the digital camera resting at Celeste's elbow. "In the meantime, how about I take a snapshot of the three of you?"

The girls huddled on either side of Dani for the photo op. Dani's smile was forced.

He wondered if there were more to this look-alike waitress situation than Dani was letting on, or was she just bothered that the man who sent the warning note might have them confused? The possibility of that worried him as well.

Beware of the dark knight.

The next time they danced, he'd have more than their swaying bodies on his mind.

DANI ABSENTLY CIRCLED HER spoon in the steaming bowl of soup a jester waiter had placed in front of her. A huge chunk of beef floated in the thick broth surrounded by onions and potatoes. This was the exact type of appetizer that would have been served to the king in merry old England, the jester had explained to the tinkling accompaniment of the bells dangling from his colorful hat.

She scanned the semicircle of tables until she spotted her near double pouring wine at a table a few yards away. She couldn't believe her eyes.

The woman was wearing the same green gown that had initiated Dani's morning fainting spell.

Her fingers slipped from the spoon, and the handle clinked against the edge of the crockery bowl. "Excuse me. I'll be right back."

Marcus jumped up, standing at the same time she did. "I'll go with you."

"No." She'd spoken too sharply. "I'm just going to say hello to a friend I've spotted a few tables away. You eat your soup while it's hot," she said, trying for a lighter tone. She walked away before he could argue the point.

Of course, he'd watch and know she'd gone to talk to the waitress, but she couldn't worry about that now. Things were finally falling into place. She knew what she had to do.

The waitress looked up as Dani approached, and when their gazes locked, Dani had that same intense sense of déjà vu she'd had this afternoon. Only this time it came with a numbing sensation of impending doom.

"I need to talk to you a moment," Dani said.

The woman backed away from her. "I can't stop now, but I'll get another waiter to assist you."

"It's personal. And urgent," Dani added quickly, when the woman looked ready to flee.

"I can't talk. I have to go back for more wine."

"This will only take a second," Dani insisted.

"Look, if this is about this afternoon, I'm sorry I bumped into you. I should have been looking where I was going."

"I didn't come for an apology."

"So what else? Are you looking to sue me for a bruised hip?"

Dani was tempted to leave. Her conscience and years of dealing with the paranormal wouldn't let her. "I'm not interested in suing, but my daughter and her friend commented on how much we resemble each other."

"If this is some kind of scheme or joke you want to play on someone, I'm not interested."

The woman was incredibly distrustful and blunt. She might very well have lots of enemies. "Someone handed me this note this afternoon," Dani explained, handing it to her. "I think it might have been intended for you."

The woman studied the scrawled writing for less than a second. Her body stiffened. "Who gave you this?"

"A teenage boy, but he said a man had given it to him and asked him to hand it to me. I think I may have seen the man this morning hanging around a shop where I was looking at a dress almost exactly like the one you're wearing now."

"What did he look like?"

"Tall, lean, dark brown hair, neatly dressed. About fifty years old, I'd guess."

The waitress returned the note to Dani. "I really need to get back to work."

"Okay," Dani said. "I just thought that you might be in danger, and I wanted to warn you."

"Well, you've done it. If I see any dark, dangerous knights, I'll run the other way." She dismissed Dani and her concerns with a wave of her hand and stalked off.

Her pretense of nonchalance disintegrated in the hurried disposal of the wine bottle into the hands of another waitress. Once her hands were free, she scanned the area nervously and walked at a near jog toward the back of the grounds.

Dani rushed after her. She was clearly upset by the note, and if she was in danger then she should talk to Marcus.

Dani tripped on her long skirt as the woman rounded one of the small buildings. "Wait," she called. "I know someone who can help."

The woman started running. So did Dani. Someone stepped from the shadows. That's when Dani saw the raised blade of the dagger poised to strike.

Chapter Five

Marcus hadn't taken his eyes off Dani for a second while she conversed with the waitress. The instant Dani chased after her, he flew into action.

He accidentally sent a waiter's tray of hot soup crashing to the ground. Everyone else cleared out of his way. He had no idea what the footrace was all about, but panic kicked in when Dani rounded the side of a timbered building and disappeared from sight.

A bloodcurdling scream cut through the

night. His body went rigid, and then something inside him snapped, releasing a burst of adrenaline that shot through every cell of his body. His reactions shifted to automatic. He pulled his weapon without slowing down.

A split-second later, he spotted Dani's moonlit silhouette, on her knees, bent over a woman sprawled in the dirt. Ever alert, he rushed to her.

"She needs an ambulance," Dani said, her voice amazingly calm. "A man stepped out from the shadows and stabbed her. I saw the whole thing."

He checked the victim's pulse, but his thoughts centered around Dani. "Are you okay?"

"Except for getting shoved to the ground while the man escaped."

The injured woman's eyes slit open. Her pulse was low, but the bigger concern was the bleeding. "Call 911," Marcus said, handing Dani his phone. "Tell them it's urgent."

He pulled off his light jacket, draped it over the

injured waitress and started administering first aid to prevent shock and slow the loss of blood.

Crowds huddled around them. Two security guards tried to keep them back once they realized Marcus knew what he was doing. Their efforts had little effect on the curious and fearful bystanders.

Dani told the security guards that she'd seen the man with the dagger. She'd jumped on his back and tried to stop him. He'd thrown her off and plunged the dagger into the woman's chest.

"Did you see where he went after that?"

"Behind that building."

One of the guards called for more help. "Why were you and the woman out here in the dark?" the other security guard asked.

Exactly what Marcus was wondering. Why hire a bodyguard and then rush into danger on her own?

"I needed to talk to her," Dani said.

"Behind a building?"

"She was running away from me. I followed her." Her voice showed signs of frustration and delayed panic.

"She'll talk to the police when they arrive," Marcus said. "You guys need to get this crowd dispersed so the ambulance can get to the victim."

"Mom!"

Dani shuddered and stood. "Over here, sweetheart."

The crowd parted enough to let Celeste through, followed by Katie and the bride-to-be. Dani took Celeste in her arms, assuring all of them she was okay. She sounded more shaken with every word that came out of her mouth.

Two of the serving crew showed up and identified the victim as Ella Somerville. They said she managed one of the festival's dress shops. Marcus noted that her blood-stained dress looked a lot like the one Dani had been looking at when she'd passed out.

He was certain Dani would have noticed that, as well.

Finally, the ambulance arrived, and Marcus surrendered his medical duties to them. The victim was still unconscious as they loaded her onto the stretcher and drove away, sirens blaring.

With luck, she'd survive this and hopefully be able to shed some light on her attacker.

Beware the dark knight.

"The cops are here!" someone shouted.

Marcus looked up to see two uniformed officers striding toward them, both looking grim. He was certain they'd give Dani the third degree. He'd see that they didn't intimidate her.

He didn't know exactly what had transpired at this point, but he was damn certain of one thing. Someone had tried to commit murder, and even if she hadn't been before, Dani was involved now.

He was not leaving her alone tonight.

A NAGGING THROB SET IN just behind both of Dani's eyes, the pain growing more severe by the second. She shifted in her seat and tried to concentrate on the last question.

She, Marcus and the deputies were seated away from the partiers. Marcus had been great, staying with her the whole time. Bethany Sue had taken Celeste and Katie back to the festivities and promised that she and Arnie would watch over them.

Dani had been answering questions for over a half hour, and the sheriff's deputies showed no sign of letting up. It was as if they thought she knew more than she was telling or that she was too upset to remember important details.

One of the deputies, Greg, was young, in his early twenties, she'd guessed. He was also the more annoying of the two, making a clicking noise with his mouth every time he didn't like her answer to one of his questions.

The tall, lanky one's name was Ted. She'd

guess him at near forty. He had sun-bleached blond hair and a scar running down the side of his face, from just below the hairline to above the eye. She stared at it and tried to imagine how he'd gotten it while he rearranged his wording for a repeat of a question.

"I can't identify the attacker," she said, "except that I'm pretty sure it was a man. It was dark, and his face was covered with one of those armored masks like the jousters wear. I've already told you all of this."

"The attacker wore armor like a knight, and you'd followed her out to warn her about a dark knight. But you don't even know this woman?"

"I know this sounds bizarre to you," she said. "It's bizarre to me, but I gave you the note."

"The note you think was meant to go to her in the first place?"

"That's just my theory of what happened. You don't seem to agree with it, but when you see the woman who was attacked, you'll realize that she looks enough like me for someone to have made that mistake."

Marcus stretched and moved his arm to the back of her chair. "Ms. Baxter was only trying to do a good deed by warning the victim. She's told you all she knows, so I can't see what's being gained by asking her the same thing over and over."

She had told them all the facts. She'd avoided any mention of nightmares and fainting spells. And she wasn't about to fuel their disbelief with talk of her being a medium.

Nonetheless, she was convinced now that the nightmare and the visions she'd witnessed this morning had to be psychic revelations. They were sent to her for a purpose. She was supposed to save Ella Somerville from the attack. She'd failed her.

Ted glared at Marcus. "We're dealing with attempted murder. That's a serious offense, and we're not going to rush any part of the investigation."

"Ms. Baxter is in town for a wedding," Marcus said. "She didn't know the victim. Other than giving you the note and telling you what she saw tonight, I don't see how she can help you solve the case."

"I'm happy to assist in any way I can," Dani offered, "but wouldn't it be more useful for you to be searching for the attackers or the murder weapon?"

"That's being taken care of." Ted rubbed his whiskered jaw. "How long do you plan to be in the area, Ms. Baxter?"

"Just long enough to attend the wedding tomorrow morning." If that long. "I plan to drive back to Austin in the afternoon."

"We'll need the number to get in touch with you there in case we have more questions."

"Certainly. I'll give you my cell phone number. You can always reach me that way."

"Then I guess that will be all for now."

She didn't have a business card with her tonight, but she gave Greg the number, and he wrote it down in his black notebook. Ted handed her his card and stressed that she call him immediately if she remembered anything else.

She sighed in relief when they finally sauntered away. "They think I'm keeping something from them."

"Are you?"

"*Et tu,* Brute?"

"I'm just asking." Marcus tugged her to her feet. "They'll check you out. If they don't see any red flags in your background, they'll move on."

"I gather parking tickets like some people do wildflowers. But I always pay them."

He smiled and snaked an arm around her shoulder. "Contributing to the department's income. That's a positive. Shall we rejoin the party?"

"Only long enough to say good-night to Bethany and drag the girls away from the festivities. I've had all the fun I can stand for one night."

"We need to talk before we get the girls."

The throb behind her eyes kicked up a notch. "I'm talked out, Marcus."

"You can trust me with anything, Dani. I want you to know that."

Right, until she hit him with the truth. "Do you think I hold some deep, dark secret that will explain who attacked the victim and why?"

"I think something's troubling you that you haven't mentioned, but that's not what we need to talk about." He took her hands in his and waited until she met his penetrating gaze. "I'm not okay with your being alone tonight."

"The note didn't refer to me. The dark knight got the prey he was after."

"You can't be sure that he has only one prey."

That she hadn't considered. Still she didn't

have much of a choice. "The B and B where we're staying is fully booked."

"Forget the B and B. I'm driving you there to collect your things, and then I'm taking you and the girls back to the ranch with me."

She looked up and saw the deep lines that were pulling at his mouth. "You're serious, aren't you?"

"Serious as a kick by a mad bull. But don't worry. This isn't some Texas seduction scene. You'll have to stay in my cabin, but you'll have your own room. The girls can stay in the main house with Cutter Martin and his wife. They're redoing the upstairs guest rooms, so they only have one extra room available at the moment."

Apparently he'd made this decision without her input. She wondered just when he'd decided that she wasn't safe on her own. While he was standing over the woman's bleeding body? While she'd described the knight plunging the dagger into the woman's chest? Or perhaps earlier, when she'd told him of the nightmare.

She hated someone else making decisions for her, but the undeniable truth was that she didn't want to be alone tonight.

"It's strictly for your protection, Dani. That is what you hired me for."

It made sense, except that spending the night with Marcus could lead to even more complications.

"Just for the night, Marcus. The girls and I will be driving back to Austin the first thing in the morning."

"What about the wedding?"

"We'll just have to miss it. Bethany Sue will surely understand." And either come up with another singer or do without music. "She might be glad to see me go, considering that the wedding excitement has already been seriously dampened by my witnessing a stabbing in the middle of her festivities."

"Judging from the music and applause going on behind us, I'd say the excitement wasn't dampened that much."

He was right. It was amazing how life went on, except for the stranger who was in a hospital now fighting for her life—if she was still alive.

A frigid chill swept through her as Marcus took her arm and led her back toward the party. He promised protection, but who could protect her from herself?

MARCUS STOOD WITH CUTTER on the front porch of the sprawling ranch house. Dani and the girls were inside. Linney was clearly delighted to have female houseguests, in spite of the fact that their reasons for being here were less than ideal.

"I guess we could put pallets on the floor for the girls if Dani wants to stay in the house with them," Cutter offered.

"Thanks, but I'd rather have her at my place."

Cutter's eyebrows arched.

"Don't give me that look, boss man. I'm not planning to jump the bones of a client."

"So what are you planning?"

"I don't know. I just figure that once she's comfortable and out of the chaos, she might open up to me."

"Then you think there's more to this than just that bizarre tale about a nightmare becoming reality?"

"I think there could be."

"Good, because I'd as soon buy that the woman was attacked by time travelers from old England as that crock. I don't know what Dani's connection is to the woman who was attacked, but I'd bet my best mare that there is one."

"It could all be coincidence," Marcus said.

"What are the odds?" Cutter leaned against the wooden porch railing. "Did you get a good look at the victim?"

"Not before she was attacked, but I was

closer to her after the stabbing than I am to you right now."

"Would you have mistaken her for Dani?"

"Probably not, but there was a definite resemblance between them. They could pass for sisters, maybe even twins if their hair was colored and styled the same."

"So you buy that Dani's receiving the note might have been a case of mistaken identity?"

Marcus thought about it hard. He was always a hundred percent honest with Cutter. "Yeah. I do, but I'm not sure that's the whole story. She appeared to be in agony when she fainted this morning. It reminded me of the way Wayne Wakefield did that first time he saw a teammate blown apart by a bomb—like he'd gone somewhere else in his mind."

Cutter nodded. "Wayne's was for real. Dani could have faked her reactions."

"For whose benefit?"

"I don't know. I'm just trying to keep an open

mind to all the possibilities. We can't get much information on Dani tonight, but I'll have her checked out fully in the morning."

Marcus knew investigating Dani was standard procedure, not to mention that it made good sense. He just didn't think Cutter would find anything criminal in her background. "She's a buyer for Duran Muton in Austin. It's not likely she's involved with an attempted murder in Plantersville."

Cutter's frown deepened. "She's a damn good-looking woman, Marcus. I hope you're not letting that cloud your judgment."

"I've got my libido under control." Not exactly true, but he wasn't planning to do anything stupid like climb into her bed tonight. Not that she'd made an offer.

"I'm not knocking your judgment," Cutter said. "I just find this whole happenstance scenario lacks credibility. All I'm saying is watch your step."

"Have you ever known me not to?"

"Not in battle. The guys used to swear you had at least six sets of eyes. You could scope out an enemy when the visibility was minus zero. But women are different. They play by their own rules of engagement."

"I'll keep that in mind."

"And don't worry about Lance Harper's kids," Cutter added. "I have a couple of excellent cops who work off-duty shifts for me in emergencies."

"I appreciate that."

The screen door screeched open and Dani stepped onto the porch. Exhaustion was sketched into the tiny lines around her eyes, and she held on to the door as if she needed it for support. Her hair was disheveled, her makeup was faded and her clothes were wrinkled. Still, she ignited some kind of crazy need inside Marcus.

He wanted to believe Dani, but her story had

more holes than his favorite jeans. A nightmare. A dress in a costume shop that created terror so real Dani had passed out. A note delivered to the wrong person. An attempted murder of a woman who could pass as her double.

There was a missing link somewhere—maybe more than one. Until he knew more, he couldn't fully trust her. And he definitely wasn't convinced that she didn't need his continued protection.

Until he was, he'd just have to keep a lid on his sexual urges, because he was not about to let her walk out of his life.

DANI STEPPED UNDER the shower spray and let the hot water cascade over her tired shoulders and run down her weary body. The muscle-binding tenseness eased, and her mind cleared to the point she could finally deal with the fact that she was spending the night in Marcus Abbot's cabin.

The place was less than a quarter the size of the sprawling main house where the girls were staying with Cutter and Linney. The furnishings were simple but functional, and they reeked of masculinity. Heavy wooden tables, big, comfortable chairs and a worn leather sofa. There were hooked cotton rugs on the floor, pastoral paintings on the walls and stacks of books, mostly mysteries, scattered everywhere.

But she'd discovered on her brief tour of the place that there were also more than a few nods to the high-tech world. A big-screen TV—for watching football, Marcus had said. And his small office at the back held a computer, fax machine, printer and shelves full of night-vision goggles and numerous instruments whose purposes she wasn't sure of. It was the only clue that Marcus was more than a cowboy.

Her assigned bedroom was on the west side of the house, down a narrow hallway from the kitchen and just opposite Marcus's sleeping quarters. The proximity would have been comforting in light of tonight's experiences if she wasn't so physically attracted to him.

Hard bodied. Unruly brown hair that crawled into the collar of his shirt, a bit shaggier than she normally liked it, but on him it looked terrific. And then there was that rugged jawline and those whiskey-colored eyes that seemed to see right through her.

To be blunt, he turned her on. And now he'd be sleeping a few steps away from her, maybe wearing nothing but that aggravatingly devastating smile.

Okay, best to rein in those thoughts right now. But when she did, her mind switched back to the sight of Ella Somerville being stabbed while she watched. An exact re-creation of the nightmare.

Dani should have followed her first instincts and stayed in Austin this weekend. But was that ever an option? Had her witnessing the vicious attack been set in place by the same paranormal powers that delivered the disturbing visions?

Perhaps she was the reason Ella was alive tonight. If Dani hadn't chased after her into the darkness, if she hadn't screamed when she did and jumped on the attacker's back, he might have stayed around long enough to make certain his victim was dead.

The concept boggled her mind.

She turned off the faucet, pushed the plastic shower curtain aside and stepped from the claw-foot tub. Her feet sank into a thick mat as she grabbed a thirsty blue towel and gave her body a brisk rubdown.

She was just slipping into her ivory-colored pajamas when she heard the soft rap at the door. Her pulse shot upward, and she checked quickly to make certain her nipples weren't outlined too vividly beneath the silky fabric. Satisfied that she was decent, she shoved her damp feet into black furry flip-flops and went to the door, opening it only a few inches.

"I found a bottle of wine. Want me to uncork it? It might help you relax."

"I'm not really dressed for a nightcap," she said.

"The clothes police are all gone for the night," he teased. "And I made sandwiches. Just ham and cheese, but all we had to eat tonight were the appetizers."

They'd missed dinner. She'd forgotten that amidst all the chaos. She wasn't hungry, but the wine sounded good. "Give me a couple of minutes, and I'll join you," she said.

"Great, but make those short minutes. I'm famished."

She ran a comb through her damp hair, rubbed some lotion onto her hands and elbows and checked her appearance in the mirror one last time. She made it to the kitchen before Marcus finished pouring the wine.

The room was warm and cozy, rife with the scents of fried ham, spicy mustard and Marcus's masculine musk. Sensual awareness skittered along her nerves as she settled into a chair across the small table from him. It was unnerving that she could have these sexual vibes after all she'd been through in the past few hours.

Marcus handed her a glass of sparkling cabernet. "To a quiet night on the Double M Ranch," he said, clinking his glass with hers.

She took a sip. The fruity liquid slid down her throat like satin. "Nice selection," she said.

"Glad you approve."

Marcus bit into his sandwich, practically inhaling it. Nothing seemed to dull his appetite. Or maybe violence and dealing with women in distress was all in a day's work for him. Yet, tonight he seemed every ounce the cowboy.

"They don't go together," she said, thinking aloud.

"Ham and cheese?"

"No, ranch life and a protection and investigative agency. One seems so settled, the other dangerous and edgy."

"I'm a complex man."

She didn't doubt that. "Did you grow up in Dobbin?"

"Nope. I'd never heard of the place until a few months ago when I went to work for Cutter Martin."

"Where did you grow up?"

"In the piney woods of east Texas, up near Longview. Cutter and I met when we were on the same team of frogmen in Afghanistan."

"You were a Navy SEAL?"

"Yep. For eight years. I was discharged last January."

"I realized you'd been in the service but not as a special ops guy. Do you miss it?"

"It's hard not to. The risks get into your blood, kind of like an addiction. But it's tough work. It wears on you after a while, but the biggest upside is that what you do as a SEAL makes a difference. Do you realize that there are areas in this world where people have never known freedom?"

Marcus shook his head, then forced a smile to his tight lips. "Now aren't you sorry you asked?"

"No." But she could see that he was, almost as if he hated that he'd let her glimpse beneath the tough outer shell he wore so well.

"Did you and Cutter plan to start this business while you were still in the service?"

"Nope. All we planned back then was staying alive and giving the enemy hell."

"Then how did the two of you end up together?"

"Cutter got hurt—nothing life threatening—but bad enough that he had to leave the SEALs before he was ready. He's only been back on the Double M for about six months, but unlike me he was never cut out to be a rancher."

"Yet he owns a ranch."

"He inherited it from his grandfather. He's the only grandson, and both his parents and his uncle are dead. His aunt Merlee had been running the place while he was away, but it got too much for her, and she'd sold off the live-stock before he took over."

"But I heard you mention to the girls that there are horses here."

"Merlee kept some horses, but none of the cattle. Originally Cutter had planned to find work in Houston. He couldn't hit upon anything to match the challenges he was used to—that is until he met Linney."

"So they've only recently married."

"Practically on their honeymoon. She was in deep trouble when he met up with her again. He barely saved her from being killed by a dirty cop. But that's a story for another night."

"So Cutter decided to start the Double M Investigation and Protection Service."

"Right," Marcus said. "To specialize in cases traditional law enforcement can't or isn't handling. He already owned the ranch, and his aunt couldn't wait to turn it over to him so it was a natural headquarters. And Linney loves the ranching life. She's already built up an impressive herd of beef cattle. So it's kind of a win-win situation for Cutter."

"But not for you?"

"It's working. It's just not my ranch."

"Were you ever married?"

"Yep, and that's definitely a story for another night."

She ate another couple of bites, then excused herself, picked up the plate with her half-eaten sandwich and carried it to the sink.

Marcus refilled their glasses. "We could take these to the front porch and catch the midnight serenade by the tree frogs and crickets."

Marcus and her alone in the moonlight. Tempting, but she doubted it was a good idea.

Soothed by the wine and the crickets, she might open up and say too much. As it was, she could drive home tomorrow and hopefully put all this behind her without openly acknowledging her psychic abilities.

Marcus reached over and tucked a lock of hair behind her ear. “I know I’ve said this a couple of times already, but you can trust me, Dani. I’m here to help, but my hands are tied when I don’t know what’s really going on.”

She stared at her feet, avoiding looking into his penetrating eyes at all costs. “I’ve told you all I know.”

“I don’t think you have.”

“Don’t try to make more of this than there is, Marcus. I got caught up in a bad situation, but it’s over, at least my part of it is. It’s in the hands of the police now.”

He trailed a finger down her arm and took her left hand in his. “I’d love to believe that.”

“Then do. I really am tired. But thanks for everything, and I'll write you a check in the morning for all your trouble."

"I don't want a check. I want to help."

Help and get dragged into her vision-haunted life where she never knew whose problems might claim her next. "Good night, Marcus." She was almost to the hallway door when the room began to spin and a frigid chill sank clear to her bones.

Her heart seemed to swell and then shrink until it floated somewhere between the walls of her chest. Excruciating stabs of pain shot through her, but it was the fear that paralyzed her. Dani swayed and reached for something to hold on to.

Two arms wrapped around her, and the haze slowly began to clear. When Dani snapped out of the trance, she tried to pull away from Marcus. He held her so tightly that she couldn't escape.

"Talk to me, Dani. Tell me what's going on with you. Tell me what happened just now." Anguish tore at his voice.

Oh, no. Why was this happening to her now?

But this time Dani was too frightened to lie to Marcus or to herself. She had to trust someone with the secret that was tearing her apart. "It's the woman. He's still going to kill her."

"How do you know?"

"I just do."

"Not good enough."

She hadn't thought that it would be. "Okay, Marcus. Let's go to the porch, and I'll try to explain. You should probably bring the rest of the wine."

Chapter Six

Moonlight filtered through the trees, adding a slivery glow to the night, a striking contrast to the tumult ripping around inside Dani. The latest vision had been vague with no clear images to define it. The fear had been all too vivid and unmistakable.

"I'll tell you everything, Marcus, but first I have to call the hospital and check on Ella Somerville. I need to know if she's alive and safe."

"I'll get the number for you," he said, leading her to a wooden porch swing. It creaked as she sat, and the noise grated along her nerves. It would take all the strength she could muster to see her through this.

Marcus connected with the nurse's desk for the ICU, then handed her the phone.

"I'm calling to check on the condition of one of your patients who was brought in tonight," she said. "Ella Somerville."

"Are you a family member?"

"Yes," she lied, afraid the truth would keep her from getting information.

"Her condition is listed as critical but stable."

"Is anyone with her?"

"Her boyfriend was here for a while. I believe he's gone now. The doctor wants her to have complete quiet for the next twelve hours. She's heavily sedated, and her vital signs are being continuously monitored. That's all I can tell you at this point. You can call back in the morning for an update."

There had been no sign of a boyfriend

when the ambulance had carried Ella away. Either the deputies or someone working the dinner party must have gotten in touch with him.

Dani took a deep breath and released it slowly. Her heart settled into a steady beat. The vision had made the danger seem imminent, but apparently Ella was safe for now.

Marcus dropped to the swing beside her, scooting close enough that she felt the brush of his thighs against hers. "Tell me what happened in the kitchen just now, Dani. The truth this time."

"You'd be better off to just drive me back to the B and B right now and forget you were ever foolish enough to hand me your card."

"Walking out on trouble's not my style." He snaked an arm across the back of the swing, letting his hand rest on her shoulder. Even in the midst of this hell, his touch stirred a hint of desire in her. If he felt the same chemistry, he'd forget it soon enough when she confessed her haunted secrets.

She swallowed and gripped the chain on the swing so hard that it cut into her palm. "You'll have to promise not to tell anyone what I'm about to tell you. That includes Cutter."

"Are you involved in something illegal or treacherous to America?"

"No. Absolutely not. It's nothing like that."

"Then I'll respect client privilege. Whatever you tell me in confidence will stay just between the two of us."

"Are you sure? This can never leak out, not even to the police, Marcus. It has potential to ruin my career and affect my daughter's happiness for the rest of her life."

"You're scaring me a bit, here. But whatever is going on with you, we'll deal with it together, in secret—with one exception."

"There can be no exceptions, Marcus."

"I can't keep a secret if it comes to the point that it risks your life."

"If it comes to that, then I guess the secret won't matter. But that's the only exception."

"Deal."

She was probably going to live to regret this, but she'd have to take Marcus at his word. She gathered all her resolve.

"I have abilities that the ordinary person doesn't have. I sense things about people, sort of like a sixth sense. Sometimes I see visions of things that either have already happened or will happen in the future unless something or someone intercedes to stop them."

Marcus removed his arm from around her neck and shifted so that he was facing her. His eyes were piercing, but confusion drew his mouth into tight, twisted lines. "Are you telling me that you're a psychic?"

"A psychic, a clairvoyant, a medium, whatever you want to call it."

"Then your nightmare was really some kind of paranormal prediction?"

"Exactly."

"And what about when you fainted?"

"I fell into a trance. The same as I did in your kitchen just now."

"How often does that happen?"

"There's no set pattern. Sometimes I go months without any type of extrasensory sensations. Other times, I get a run of psychic activity."

"The way you are now?"

"Yes, except this is far more intense than what I'm used to. I've never fainted while in a trance before today. Normally if someone's with me, they just think I'm daydreaming or that my mind's somewhere else—which it is."

"Is intensity the only difference this time?"

"No. The violence is new for me, as is having strangers involved. Those aren't unusual psychic phenomena in and of themselves, but they are new for me."

She was saying far more than she'd intended to, but talking about it after so many years of denial felt strangely cathartic. Marcus's reaction helped, too. He seemed to take what she was saying as a statement of fact, seemed more intrigued than judgmental.

"I know I'm asking a lot of questions here," Marcus said, "but this is all Greek to me. I'm just trying to wrap my mind around it."

"Go ahead. I've said this much. There's no reason for me to hold back now."

"In that case, what kinds of things would you normally see in a trance?"

"Problems or illnesses involving my friends."

"For instance?"

She tried to think of one that was fairly typical. "Last year the mother of one my coworkers, a lady named Janice, was planning to marry a man she'd connected with on an Internet dating service. When I met the man at a dinner party at Janice's house, I picked up disturbing vibes. That night I had a series of short visions in which I saw him with several other women, all widowed and financially well off, as was Janice's mother."

"How did you handle that without admitting to the visions?"

"With a white lie. I told Janice I'd seen a TV special where a charming, intelligent man courted widows he'd met over the Internet and bilked them out of their savings. I encouraged her to have her mother's boyfriend investigated. Luckily, she took my advice."

Marcus leaned forward and rested his elbows on his knees. "You're the first psychic I've ever met."

The truth was out. After years of keeping her bizarre abilities secret, Dani had finally confessed to possessing them. To a perfect stranger, no less.

Marcus left the swing and paced the porch for a few minutes before finally perching on the railing a few feet away from her. “How about starting with the nightmare and telling me everything you’ve seen or felt since then so that I have clear picture of what we’re dealing with?”

She did, ending with the vague trance in his kitchen where all she could make out was that Ella was not only in pain but deathly afraid.

“I don’t understand why I’ve been linked with Ella Somerville in such intense fashion,” Dani said, “but I know I’m supposed to help her. I just don’t know how.”

“You helped her tonight, probably even kept her from being killed.”

“But she may still be in danger, so I can’t walk away from her. I know you didn’t buy into this, Marcus. If you think I’m a basket case or just don’t want to get involved with a psychic, you can walk away from me and the situation in the morning.”

He met her gaze head-on. “Let’s get a couple of things straight here. First, I don’t think you're a basket case. I think you're a strong, gutsy woman. Second, I'm not walking anywhere without you. Once I start something, I *never* give up until the mission is completed. Now, just tell me one more thing."

"Make it easy."

"You said that you didn't see the victim clearly in the original nightmare, but in the trance this morning in the shop, was it Ella you saw, or was it you?"

"I was afraid it was me at the time, but I was wrong. It had to have been Ella. The trance predicted her stabbing." She couldn't go through this again tonight. "I'm exhausted. I'd really like to go to bed now." Hopefully not to dream.

He stood, took her hand and tugged her to her feet. "I think we should go to the wedding tomorrow, Dani. You and the girls, just like you'd planned. Only I'll go with you."

"I've had quite enough of the Renaissance

festival, and I don't see how attending the wedding will help Ella."

"I might learn something there that I can't learn from the police report or a background check on Ella Somerville."

It was clear he wasn't going to just let go of this. And if he thought she was a kook, he was hiding it well. "I'll think about it, Marcus."

"Good enough." He walked with her to her bedroom door, stopping when they reached it and propping a hand against the frame. "I'll be right across the hall if you need me for anything, anything at all."

His voice had grown husky. She swallowed hard, suddenly all too aware of how close he was standing. The air between them crackled with tension and sparks of desire.

He leaned nearer, and his lips brushed hers. A feathered touch that was over all too quickly.

Her pulse skyrocketed as she slipped inside the door and closed it behind her. It could hardly count as a kiss at all, any more than the brushing of their lips earlier could. But this time it resonated through her whole body.

She'd witnessed an attempted murder and trusted a stranger with the most closely held secret of her life. Yet here she was awed by the mere touch of Marcus's lips on hers.

That might well be the strangest and most frightening event of the day.

BETHANY SUE CLAIMED the attention she deserved in an exquisite ivory satin and lace strapless gown that narrowed at the waist before swirling into a flouncing froth of a skirt and a lace-trimmed train. The style was more timeless than Elizabethan, but the rest of the attendants and the groom had strictly adhered to the Renaissance dictates.

Arnie was positively dashing in black pants that gathered around the top of knee-high black leather boots. His shirt was the exact creamy tint as Bethany's gown with full sleeves and a soft fabric that draped loosely over his broad shoulders. The enameled and jeweled sword at his side was the crowning touch of authenticity. No lord of the court could have looked more swashbuckling.

The ceremony went off without a hitch on a glorious Texas autumn day. In spite of her earlier worries, Dani managed to stay somewhat on key during the two songs Bethany had chosen for the ceremony.

The knot had now been officially tied, and the groom had quite nobly kissed the bride. Celeste and Katie were flitting around the attendees, relishing the attention they were getting in their fairy costumes and accidentally bumping guests with their unruly silver wings.

Dani let down her guard a bit for the first time since she'd arrived at the festival a little over twenty-four hours ago. Still, she was ready to get back in her car and head toward

Austin. She'd decided that keeping Ella safe called for more expertise than she possessed. She had a great idea for how to deal with that.

She wasn't eager to leave Marcus behind, but once she was back at work, she'd put him and the uncanny sensual urges he ignited to rest—or at least to a comfortable spot at the back of her mind.

She turned at a tap to her shoulder, expecting it to be Marcus and thankful that her heart hadn't flipped at his nearness.

"Can I talk to you a minute, somewhere quieter?"

She found herself staring into the troubled eyes of a woman whose facial features were completely hidden by a purple feathered mask. Dani grew instantly wary. "What do you want to talk about?"

"Ella Somerville."

Dani's anxiety level heightened tenfold. "What about her?"

The woman looked around nervously before turning back to Dani. "The man who stabbed her is going to kill Ella unless someone stops him."

"Have you told this to the sheriff?"

"I can't."

No need to ask why. The woman was afraid to even be seen talking to Dani. The mask and her hurried, whispered voice made that obvious. Dani spotted Marcus a few feet away, deep in conversation with Arnie's best man. He'd ordered her not to leave the immediate area without him.

She didn't take orders well. Nor was she taking any chances like she had last night when she'd left the partiers and chased after Ella. "We can talk over there, behind that hedge," she said, pointing to one of the manicured bushes that bordered the outdoor wedding chapel.

The woman nodded and followed her. They

were out of sight of most of the guests but still only steps away from Marcus. Dani wasted no time on formalities. "Do you know who attacked Ella?"

"No."

"Then what makes you think she's in danger?"

"I just know that she is."

Could this be another psychic? Dani doubted it. "Why are you telling me this?"

"You're her sister. Don't you want to help her?"

"I'm not kin to Ella. I don't even know her."

"But…"

"I know. We look alike. It's purely coincidental. Yesterday was the first time I'd ever seen Ella."

The woman glanced at her watch, one with jeweled dragons for hands. "I've got to go. Just talk to the police, and make sure they know Ella's still in danger."

"At least tell me your name."

"Dani." It was Marcus's voice, tinged with anxiety.

She stepped from behind the hedge. "Over here." When she turned back to the woman, she'd vanished.

Marcus walked over and stood beside her. "You look upset? Is something wrong?"

"Just more of the weekend from hell."

His eyebrows arched questioningly.

"I'll explain later." When she figured out exactly what she was going to do with this new information.

Marcus slipped his arms around her waist. "I haven't had a chance to tell you, but you sounded great up there crooning those romantic ballads. You didn't tell me you could sing."

"And now that you've heard me, you know why."

"You could sing me to sleep any night."

Marcus. The truth hit her like a thunderbolt. He was the reasoning behind all of this. She should have realized it from the beginning. He hadn't dropped into her life for her protection. He was here for Ella's. It wasn't just any bodyguard Dani should hire.

That should make it easier to walk away from him in a few minutes and head back to Austin on her own. It still wouldn't be easy, not with him looking at her like she was the topping on a sundae and just waiting to be devoured.

He trailed a finger down her cheek, letting it stop at her lips.

She struggled for breath. "I have a proposition for you, Marcus."

"I thought you'd never ask."

Chapter Seven

"I want to hire you to protect Ella Somerville."

Dani's statement did serious damage to Marcus's ego. He dropped his hands to his sides. "Is that your solution for getting rid of me?"

"No. I was getting rid of you anyway. Wait, that didn't come out the way I meant it to." She took a deep breath and exhaled slowly. "I'm going back to Austin this afternoon. I definitely don't need protection there, but I think Ella might."

"She may," Marcus agreed, "but I can't take her on."

"Why not?"

"I have a woman to protect in Austin. I'm good, but I can't be in two places at once."

She put her hands out, palms up and looked at him with those expressive, pleading eyes that could have melted an iceberg. "My hiring you was a mistake, Marcus. I never needed protection. It was Ella Somerville who was in danger. I misread the visions, but they're perfectly clear now. I'll pay you your standard protection rate. What is it, by the way?"

"The price is negotiable. If you want to hire protection for Ella, I'll arrange it, either with Cutter or with a bodyguard service out of Houston, but I'm going to Austin. End of argument."

She crossed her arms in front of her and struck a stubborn stance. "I'm not in danger, Marcus. What part of that don't you get?"

"The part where you're wearing a green

velvet ball gown and someone pushes a dagger into your heart."

"But it wasn't *me.* It was just a woman who looked like me."

"In that case, I won't charge overtime."

Her cheeks grew red. "If this is your idea of finding a way to get into my bed, it isn't going to work."

Exactly the kind of accusation he'd expected when he'd made his decision. He had the argument for that. "You're sexy, intelligent and spunky, Dani—all the qualities that I like in a woman. And if you want me in your bed, all you have to do is wiggle a finger in my direction. But that's not why I'm following you to Austin."

"You won't like my town house. It's in the center of the business area, not on a ranch."

"I doubt we'll be spending a lot of time there."

"You're definitely not following me to Duran Muton, Marcus Abbot."

He adjusted his sunglasses. "We'll work out the details later."

She groaned and marched away from him. She was furious, but he'd won the argument. That would do for now. He wasn't psychic, but his instincts for pending disaster had never betrayed him.

His cell phone rang. He took the call. It was Cutter.

"I have some information on Ella Somerville."

"Fast work," Marcus said.

"I had help from Eduardo, best tech man in the business."

Cutter was lucky the guy was available for part-time research whenever they needed him. "Does Ella have a rap sheet?"

"Not as Ella Somerville, but that could be an alias."

"How's that?"

"The Ella Somerville whose social security number was used at the hospital has been dead for two years. Not sure how Ella got the number, but she has a Missouri driver's license under the same information."

"Were you able to find any employee records?"

"Nothing."

Marcus pulled a black notebook from his back pocket and started scribbling notes. "What about her current stats?"

"She manages one of the dress shops and has been traveling the Renaissance circuit and living with one of the jousters for the past few months. The guy's name is Kevin Flanders."

"Did you run a check on him?"

"It's in the works. Early feedback indicates he may be operating under a fake name as well."

"Have the police learned anything new from Ella?"

"She hasn't spoken to them at all as yet. The doctor says she's not responding to verbal stimuli, meaning she may be scared to talk. At least that's how I read that. What about you? Did you pick up any info from the wedding guests?"

"Pretty much the same, except that I also heard that Kevin, or Kev as he's known around here, is hotheaded and likes to gamble. A friend of the best man who also travels the festival route says Kev tried to borrow five hundred dollars from him a few weeks ago. When he told him no, Kevin made some threats of violence. The guy didn't take him seriously."

"Not sure why Ella would want to follow him around the country but there is nothing there to tie him to trying to kill her," Cutter noted.

"No, but someone wanted her dead, which leads me to one other complication. Dani wants me to protect Ella until the perpetrator is arrested."

"What did you tell her?" Cutter asked.

"That I already had a job. It took some convincing, but I think she's finally accepted that I'm going back to Austin with her until there's an arrest or we get a better handle on the situation and know she's safe."

"Why would Dani assume responsibility for the safety of a virtual stranger?"

"I'm not sure. Something to do with seeing her stabbed, I think." He was really uncomfortable not giving Cutter the full truth. He'd talk with Dani about that. Client privilege shouldn't rule out his being able to discuss the business of her protection with his boss and confidant.

"I'd take on Ella's protection for her," Cutter said, "but I'm meeting with a bigwig from Homeland Security tomorrow afternoon regarding a top-secret investigation of drug dealers in Texas border towns."

"Covert, dangerous and going after the bad guys. That sounds right up your alley."

"Yeah. I'm hoping we can come to an agreement, meaning he's going to let me run my own show my way. But there are plenty of good agencies in Houston that can supply a bodyguard if Ms. Somerville agrees to the arrangement. I'm not sure that she will, considering she's not talking to the cops."

Marcus spotted Dani off to his right, in a circle of people standing near the rose-bedecked altar. From the looks of the hugging going on, she was bidding the bride and groom farewell. "I've got to run, but I'll keep you posted if I learn anything new, and you do the same."

They broke the connection, and Marcus stood for a minute watching Dani. The sun lit her hair with streaks of gold, and her smile was devastating in spite of all she'd been through. Damn. He had to get past this attraction.

The woman had only been in his life for a little more than twenty-four hours and already she had him panting after her. He couldn't remember any woman crawling under his skin that fast.

It could be the intrigue and danger she brought to the relationship, or maybe just that she was such a fascinating mix of sophistication and warmth, of secrets and vulnerability. Or it could be that she was a knockout with her fabulous body, cute nose, full lips and expressive eyes.

Hell, it was all of that, but he'd keep his libido in check if it took a dozen cold showers a day. He was here to protect, not to seduce. And the last thing he needed was to fall for a city girl like Dani, who probably had a dozen Austin businessmen fawning all over her. His heart wasn't up to being stomped on again.

On the other hand, one night with Dani might be worth the pain.

THE GIRLS DRIPPED glittery fairy dust as they maneuvered their unwieldy wings into the backseat of Marcus's truck. They were talking a mile a minute, mostly about the festival.

It wasn't that they were insensitive to Ella Somerville's plight—they'd asked about her as soon as they'd woken this morning. But the Renaissance wedding had been unique and exciting for them and pretty much pushed last night's violence from their minds. Dani envied them for that.

She hadn't told them yet that Marcus would be going back to Austin with them and staying in the guest room for a few days. Needless to say, Celeste would be thrilled. He'd won her over the second she'd found out he lived on a ranch with horses. Both she and Katie had already finagled invitations to return to the Double M for a short vacation next summer.

Dani was still dubious about Marcus's insistence to be her protector. She was flattered by his concern, but the chemistry between them grew more combustible by the second. This wasn't supposed to happen to people her age. Not that she was old at thirty-three, but she was well past the instant-infatuation stage.

Only it was happening.

Marcus slid behind the wheel of his truck. "Ready to roll?"

Celeste pulled off her worse-for-wear wings, accidentally bouncing them off the back of Marcus's head in the process. "Sorry. I don't think fairies are supposed to ride in trucks."

"Maybe they ride horses," Marcus said.

"Ooh. Lucky fairies," Celeste crooned. "Can we go horseback riding before we drive back to Austin?"

"Yeah, can we?" Katie added. "Puh-leeze. We don't have school tomorrow so we don't have to do homework or go to bed early."

"I'll be glad to take you riding," Marcus said, "but you'll have to clear it with Dani."

The chorus of pleading was louder than the crickets had been last night. They didn't have school tomorrow due to a teacher's conference, but she did have work. Still, another hour or two wouldn't put them home all that late.

"You love to ride, Mom," Celeste said. "And

you won't have to follow that same old trail that you think is so boring when we go to the stable near our house."

"I didn't bring riding clothes."

Marcus pulled onto the highway. "You can borrow some old jeans from Linney. In fact, since the girls don't have school tomorrow, the three of you could just stay over another night. We can build a fire out back and roast wieners and marshmallows."

That bought a whoop and holler from the girls. Marcus was not making this easy. But if she stayed, it would likely mean her spending the night again in the cozy cabin with Marcus. No chaperones. No one to know if he kissed her again. No one to know if the temptation grew out of control and she ended up in his bed.

Her insides started to melt at the thought.

Marcus nudged his black hat back a few inches, letting a lock of dark hair fall over his forehead. "If you'd like, we can drive to the hospital in The Woodlands after the horseback ride. You can talk to Ella Somerville and see for yourself how she's doing."

Now that was dirty pool.

Marcus knew she couldn't turn down that offer and wondered why she hadn't thought of it herself.

If Ella was still in as much danger as the masked lady predicted, then she should be glad to accept Dani's offer of protection. Even better, if her boyfriend, Kevin Flanders, was there and she could see him in person, she might pick up an extrasensory indicator as to whether or not he was behind the attack.

"Please, Mom." Celeste leaned forward and put her hands on the back of Dani's seat. "Let's stay another night on the ranch. Linney might even let us help with the horses in the morning like we did today."

"You can go horseback riding, and I'll think about spending the night," she said, though the more she thought about it, the better the idea seemed.

She didn't have any appointments or meetings tomorrow, so it wouldn't be much of a sacrifice to take a vacation day. She considered Marcus's offer.

A horseback ride with a man who could heat her blood with a look and a trip to the hospital all but invited more disturbing visions into her mind. Dani wasn't sure which frightened her most.

THE GALLOPING RIDE ACROSS sun-drenched pastures and along shady, wooded trails proved the perfect antidote for the worries and stress that clogged Dani's mind. Her lungs expanded to take in the brisk, clean air, and her spirits lifted to exhilarating levels.

She might have gone on like this for hours. The horses shouldn't. They stopped to rest them beside a meandering river that cut through a forested area. Marcus slid to the ground, looped the reins of his magnificent steed and walked over to help Dani and the girls dismount.

"Look, there's a doe," Celeste called.

The doe looked up, froze for a second and then darted back into the brush.

"You frightened it away," Katie said.

"You'll see more," Marcus said. "This is a popular late-afternoon gathering spot for the herd."

Two squirrels scurried across the carpet of pine straw a few feet away and then chased each other up a towering pine tree. A crow squawked at them from a lofty branch.

Dani stepped around an ant bed. "Nature is alive and well on the Double M."

"Yep, the good and the bad," Marcus said, swatting a horsefly.

"Can we take a walk along the creek?" Celeste asked.

"You can," Marcus said, "but that's actually Martin River, named after and by Cutter's great-grandpa when he settled here."

"That little stream of water is a river?"

"Right on. It doesn't look like much now, but it sometimes overflows the banks when the spring rains set in. It's full of fish."

"And turtles," Celeste said. "I just saw a big one slide off that log and into the water."

Celeste and Katie started walking, following the twisting bank of the rippled waterway.

"Don't get lost," Dani called after them. "And don't be gone too long."

"Let them explore," Marcus said. "It's good for the soul, and there's nowhere they can go that I can't track them in a matter of minutes."

"Sure of yourself, aren't you?"

"About some things." Marcus stooped, picked up a pebble and tossed it into the water. "I worked and trained with the best."

"How do you train for a special operations

unit? From what I've heard the tasks you're called to do are extremely diverse."

"The training is just as diverse and more intense than most people can imagine. And it isn't just about water operations. SEAL stands for sea, earth and land, the elements in which frogmen operate."

Marcus kicked away a few pinecones next to the base of a thick-trunked tree. He sat down, stretched out his legs and patted a spot next to him. "Room for one more."

She hesitated, then dropped down beside him. A heated flush swept through her as her jean-clad thighs rubbed against his. "Were you pleased when they assigned you to SEAL training?"

"You're not assigned. You volunteer, and you can back out anytime you decide you can't take it. You just ring out and go."

"Ring out?"

"Yeah. There's a bell. You're free to ring out

anytime, twenty-four hours a day. A lot of guys in my class did."

"But not you?"

"I knew what I wanted and was determined to make the grade. But it was tough. Seven hundred push-ups before breakfast was just a starter. So was running miles in the sand and doing calisthenics until the sweat caked on you like mud, or walking into the surf with a telephone pole on your back. And if you messed up you got to dip in the cold Pacific waters and roll in the sand. Then you got to spend the rest of the day wet and sandy."

"It sounds like torture."

"Seemed that way, too, at the time. But in the end, the BUDS training is what ensures that every SEAL team member is able to pull his weight and do the job he's assigned in any type of climate or terrain and in any situation. It's also why I don't believe in giving up."

Marcus Abbot, cowboy at heart, had passed

all the tests. He was a man among men, yet sitting beside him on this glorious fall afternoon as the sun slid to the horizon, she sensed he was much more than muscle, brawn and determination.

He caught her hand in his. “Do I sound like a blowhard?”

“Not at all. What was it like in the heat of battle?”

“Every battle is different. We worked as a team, and we were always so focused on the action and what was required of each of us that there wasn’t much time for thinking of anything else. It was the quiet hours when we were waiting for the danger that I remember most. That’s when I had time to look at my life and figure out what really matters to me.”

“What does matter to you, Marcus?”

“Being true to myself. I’m a simple man. I want to own a ranch, not necessarily a big one, but one where I can raise cattle and horses and have wide-open spaces to roam."

"No wife and houseful of kids?"

"They're not in the picture at the moment."

"No Double M I and P?"

"At some point, I'll be ready to give it up. I've had a lot of adventures as a SEAL, but I'm just your average cowboy. What you see is what you get."

He saw himself as a simple man. She saw him as extremely complicated. Intelligent, strong, brave, honest. Modest. A hero in every sense of the word. Not the kind of man a woman could walk away from easily. Yet someone had.

"You said you were married once. What happened with that?"

"Too many lonely nights, I guess. I came home thinking we'd buy a ranch and start a family. She'd started without me."

"She was pregnant?"

He nodded. "By a friend of mine who'd

promised to look after her while I was out of the country."

"Some friend." And some wife, though Dani didn't voice that sentiment. But his wife had been the real loser, walking out on a man like Marcus. It was difficult to imagine any sane woman doing that.

"It must be tough to bounce back from that type of betrayal," she said. Actually, she knew it was. She'd been there, too. Only her ex had a much better reason for walking out on her.

"Our breakup was probably inevitable," Marcus said. "Tyrone was there. I wasn't. It's not quite as easy to forgive the fact that she'd blown all our savings on expensive clothes to impress him or on fancy trips for the two of them."

"Ouch. Talk about a low blow."

"You got it. It put the skids on my buying a ranch, but I'll get there eventually. In the meantime I have the Double M and a job that's getting more interesting by the second."

Marcus let go of her hand and shifted so that he faced her. She met his smoldering gaze, and the inhibitions that controlled so much of her life went up in smoke. She touched his whiskered chin with her fingertips, then traced a line to his waiting lips. Her heart skipped to a ragged rhythm. If he didn't kiss her, she was going to have to kiss him.

But his mouth found hers, and the thrill ripped through her, awakening every part of her body. When she parted her lips and felt the quick thrust of his tongue, her insides quaked from the intensity of her emotions. For the first time she could see how a person could drown in desire.

She ached for air, yet couldn't bear to pull away. When Marcus did, the separation of their mingled breaths was almost painful.

"The girls. They're coming back," he added when the truth of the situation didn't sink in fast enough.

Dani jumped to attention, turning away from

Marcus and covering her mouth with her hand as if her lips would give her away.

"We should be going," she said, when the girls tramped into sight. The hoarseness of passion tinged her voice, but the girls didn't seem to notice.

Marcus took the lead, jumping to his feet and extending a helping hand to her. In minutes they were back in the saddles. Everything was as before, except now there was no way to deny the raw sensual hunger he incited.

But it was more than just physical need. It was passion. Frightening, mind-numbing, breath-stealing passion. And the kiss had only touched the edges of it.

DANI AND MARCUS absentmindedly thumbed through magazines in the waiting room, waiting for the clock on the wall to hit 7:00 p.m., the designated time for visiting ICU patients.

The kiss still dominated Dani's mind in spite

of her efforts to push it aside. It had rocked her soul, and when she touched her fingertips to her lips, she could swear she still felt its heat.

Marcus showed no sign that it affected him in the same way. He'd been cool to her since the kiss, avoiding meeting her gaze or touching her in any way.

It hurt, but she didn't blame him. He knew what he wanted from life. A psychic who slipped into trances without warning and got pulled into other people's danger wasn't it. The kiss had likely brought that home to him. Better for him to back off before he started something that might be difficult to stop.

Finally the reality that she'd see Ella in a matter of minutes began to sink in. Her hands grew clammy. Her stomach churned.

She'd seen Ella twice before, and each time the feeling that she knew Ella from somewhere had been incredibly strong. Yet she had no clear recollection of ever having crossed paths with the woman. If this was part of the psychic experience, it was a new and unfamiliar dimension.

The most important thing was for Dani not to let their meeting push her into a trance while she was in the ICU. She needed to talk to Ella and assure her that she'd be protected, not frighten her more.

The hour hand inched toward the twelve, and a petite nurse with short black hair opened the door and waved the visitors into the unit.

"Are you family?" the nurse asked when Dani and Marcus reached the door.

"No, just friends. I was with her last night before the attack." That was all the information Dani offered. Any more and she'd probably be denied permission to visit.

"Good. It might help for Ms. Somerville to hear a familiar voice. Her recovery is remarkable, and her vital signs are strong. She may even be moved into a semiprivate room tomorrow morning if she continues to improve. The main concern now is that she's unresponsive much of the time. It could be the result of the violence."

The nurse walked with them to Ella's bedside. "Talk quietly," she cautioned. "Hopefully she'll respond, but don't say anything to upset her. I'll be nearby if you need me."

Dani stared at the pale woman lying beneath the bleached white sheets. Breathing tubes carried oxygen into her nostrils. An IV was attached to her right arm, and she was hooked to a monitor that measured every heartbeat.

The same powerful sense of déjà vu attacked again, and Dani clutched the bed rail to keep her hands from shaking.

"Hello," she whispered, leaning in close so that only Ella could hear her words. "I'm Dani Baxter. We crossed paths yesterday at the festival and again last night just before you were attacked."

Ella opened her eyes but turned her face to

the wall as if she didn't realize Dani was standing there.

"I want to help you."

No response.

"A friend of yours came to see me today. She thinks you may still be in danger."

The muscles in Ella's face twitched. Dani was almost positive she heard and understood.

"I'm hiring a bodyguard to stay with you until you get back on your feet and are able to handle the situation yourself. And I'm putting my card on the table by your bed. Call me when you feel like talking."

Finally the woman turned and faced Dani. "I don't want your help," she whispered through clenched teeth. "Stay out of this. Stay out of my life."

Her words were harsh, but it was the terror in her haunted eyes that made Dani's blood run cold. "I just want to help. You don't owe…"

"Get away or he'll kill you, too." Ella slung

the arm with the IV attached into the bed railing on the opposite side from where Dani was standing. The loud clunk brought the nurse instantly.

The IV was still in place, but Ella's body jerked spastically beneath the sheets.

"You'll have to go now," the nurse said. "We need to calm the patient." A second nurse appeared at Dani's elbow to lead her away from the bed. Dani slid her business card next to Ella's water glass.

Marcus put a hand to the small of her back as they left the hospital.

"Ella Somerville knows exactly what's going on," Dani said as they approached the truck. "She's just horribly afraid. I felt it and saw it in her eyes."

"Maybe, but she made things perfectly clear," Marcus said. "She wants you out of her life, and she thinks you'll be in danger if you don't abide by those wishes."

"It's not like I asked to get involved with her. Some unearthly spirit with a rotten sense of humor dragged me into her problems with that dratted nightmare and those incongruous visions."

"Let it go, Dani. You did what you could. It's out of your hands. Let's go home and leave Ella's problems to the police."

She sucked in a jagged breath. "My home's in Austin, and I don't think I have the energy to drive that far tonight."

"We've already discussed this. You have a bedroom in mine."

A bedroom but no suggestion that she share his. Ella was not the only one making things perfectly clear.

Chapter Eight

The campfire was blazing by the time Dani and Marcus returned to the ranch, the odors from sizzling wieners and toasty marshmallows drifting through the air with the sparkling embers.

The girls ran to meet them with news of their own. "My mom says I can stay the night," Katie said, "as long as I'm back home for bedtime tomorrow night."

"And Linney says we can ride again and help with the horses tomorrow morning,"

Celeste added. "So, please don't make us go home tonight."

Dani looked to Linney for assurance the invitation was genuine.

"I love having them here," Linney said. "So do the horses. They've never had so much attention. And Cutter will be gone most of the day tomorrow. It can get a tad lonesome out here when it's just me, Eddie and the animals around."

"Who's Eddie?" Dani asked, feeling a bit out of the loop.

"Eddie Johnson is our foreman and almost family. He's worked at the Double M for years."

"I'm sorry I haven't met him."

"He's away for the weekend," Cutter said, "visiting a new grandson up in Fort Worth."

"Is Eddie it," Dani asked, "or do you have other people working on the ranch?"

"He's it for now," Linney said. "But I've been negotiating with a couple of wranglers from El Paso who may start working here in the spring.

If they do, we'll have to update that old bunkhouse. And I think Cutter may have found another former special ops guy for his business."

Marcus stepped away from the fire where he'd been warming his backside and hands. "I hadn't heard that."

"I got a call from Hawk Taylor today. He heard about our operation and he's interested."

"Hawk? In quiet little Dobbin, Texas? This I gotta see." The men exchanged high fives.

"Maybe I should meet this man before you hire him," Linney said.

"So, Mom, can we stay the night?" Celeste asked again, turning the conversation back to her own interests in true preteen fashion.

"We can and we are. I'm too exhausted to risk driving home on dark country roads tonight."

"Does that mean we can stay long enough to go riding again in the morning, too? Please, Ms. Baxter. Please."

"I don't see why not."

The girls squealed their delight and went back to roasting marshmallows and warming themselves at the open blaze.

Dani took her plate over to sit by Linney at the patio table while Marcus and Cutter found a quiet spot near the freestanding garage to eat and chat, no doubt about their visit with Ella. The two men seemed an inseparable team where work was involved.

Dani wasn't sure exactly what Marcus had shared about her with his boss, but she trusted that he hadn't mentioned the psychic abilities that he'd sworn to keep secret. All indications were that he was a man of his word.

Besides, if Cutter and Linney knew the truth about her, she doubted they'd still be welcoming her to the ranch with open arms. More likely they'd be warning Marcus to keep her at a distance.

Apparently he'd come to that conclusion on his own. Too bad he hadn't made that decision before he'd kissed her. Before desire had rocked through her every cell. Before she'd ached for fulfillment. Before she'd…

"Dani?"

She jerked from her reverie, her cheeks burning at being caught entertaining such sensual thoughts. Fortunately, it was too dark in the firelight for Linney to see her embarrassment.

"I'm sorry. I didn't get much sleep last night, and I'm fading fast. Did you ask me a question?"

"Nothing important. I'm just curious about your job as a formal wear buyer. It sounds fascinating."

"It is, especially my trips to market."

"Are those in Dallas?"

"Yes, and New York, London and Paris. Duran Muton caters to the wealthy and fashionable, but we specialize in tasteful, classic styles."

"You do a great job with that. I know. I've shopped there—when I was married to my first husband. He liked me in the sexiest designs imaginable, but I preferred the classic look. You'd think I'd miss my extravagant shopping excursions, wouldn't you?"

"Do you?"

"Not really. I had my fill of being a socialite. I love my life on the ranch, but to tell you the truth I'd be happy anywhere as long as I was with Cutter. I'm absolutely crazy in love with him."

"It shows. He obviously feels the same about you."

"We were meant to be." Linney fingered her wedding band. "I don't mean to be nosy, but I get the feeling today that you and Marcus have a little chemistry going on, as well."

"I don't. We haven't…" Dani stumbled over her words like a drunk. "What I meant to say is we barely know each other."

"Sometimes that's all it takes. Marcus will make a great husband for the woman who's able to rein him in."

That wouldn't be Dani. She looked around for Marcus. He was still deep in conversation with Cutter, but when he caught her eye, he nodded. In less than a minute, he was by her side and announcing that it was time for them to settle in at his cabin.

No one questioned that she was spending the night with him there, not even the girls. Dani and Marcus were responsible adults, and his cabin housed the only spare bedroom.

Chemistry or not, she'd sleep in it alone tonight.

THICK LAYERS OF BLACK CLOUDS had blown in, obscuring the moon and stars. Marcus skulked through the house in the pitch dark, as silent as if he were in enemy territory. He couldn't sleep, but he didn't want to wake Dani with his rambling.

Cutter had warned him not to let his emotions get tangled up with his determination to protect

Dani. He'd thought he could handle the attraction, but he'd proved today he couldn't.

It had been all he could do not to take her right there in the woods like some beast. He'd been that turned on. If the girls hadn't been with them, who knows what might have happened.

Now guilt had him feeling like a barbarian. Dani was vulnerable, dealing with a barrage of paranormal trances and visions that had her afraid and confused. Not so much for herself as for the woman who'd come out of her fake unconsciousness only to snarl at Dani—and to warn that she, too, could be in danger.

He knew the rules of engagement as well as Cutter. Keep a clear mind and focus at all times when there is a possibility of danger.

But the kiss had definitely changed things. He'd known the attraction was there, but he hadn't anticipated that that level of fire and raw, animalistic hunger could be brought on by a kiss.

It was as if they'd both erupted with

passion, giving in to desires as basic as breathing, as overwhelming as a tidal wave. She was a contradiction—yielding, yet demanding. Her soft pliant body, fitting against his. Her sensual energy as electric as direct current.

Just thinking about her was getting him worked up again. He didn't see how a man could ever get enough of a woman like Dani. Yet some jerk had walked out on her. The world was full of lunatics.

Like the lunatic who'd attacked Ella Somerville last night.

The wind picked up and the first drops of rain started to fall. A cold front was coming in. Weather made for snuggling against a warm, supple, seductive body. And if he kept thinking like this he'd never make it through the night without tasting Dani's full, sweet lips again.

That was a mistake he planned to avoid.

THE GOWN WAS EXQUISITE, jade velvet with delicate white lace at the neckline and peeking from under the laced corset and below the hemline. The waist was tiny, the skirt billowing. It was fit for a queen. Or a burial.

"No, please, don't. You've made a mistake."

"There's no mistake. Did you really think changing your name and the color of your hair would make you unrecognizable?"

"I'm not Ella."

"I know, my sweet Helena. You forget how well I know you. You could never be an Ella. Now stop whining, and put on the dress."

"I won't."

He slapped her across the face so hard she stumbled backward and fell against the wall. She tried to run, but he grabbed her arm and pulled her to him. "We can make this as bloody and as painful as you like, or you can behave like the lady you used to be."

"Get your hands off me."

He hit her again, this time with his fist. When she fell to the floor, her head cracked against the leg of the sofa. He put a fist in her stomach, then unbuttoned her jeans and tore them from her body. The panties were the next to go. Then her shirt and her bra, not stopping until she was stripped naked.

"Put on the dress, Helena. Put on the dress for me, the way you wear it for your drunken lover."

"I'm not Ella."

He lifted a pearl-handled dagger above her, its blade pointed at her chest. "Put on the dress."

She retched and choked on the blood that was dripping from her mouth. She tried to scream, but she was choking on the warm, sticky river trickling down her throat.

His hands lifted her bruised and bleeding body and pulled the dress over her head.

"Make love to me the way you've made love to him, Helena. Make love to me. And then you die."

THE SOFT GURGLING in the wee hours of the morning wakened Marcus. He never slept soundly. His hearing was as fine-tuned as the rest of him, like a machine programmed to detect every change in the environment.

He jerked to a sitting position. The noise sounded like a muted coughing or as if someone were choking. Adrenaline galloped through his veins. A heartbeat later, he was rushing toward Dani's bedroom, his weapon on ready.

He shoved the door open and pushed inside. Dani was in the middle of the bed, squirming frantically, fighting the covers. The front of her white pajamas were wet with perspiration.

Her eyes were open, but his presence hadn't seemed to register with her. She was deep in a trance, and whatever she was seeing was killing her.

"It's okay, Dani. I'm here."

He crossed the room, dropped to the side of the bed and took her shuddering body in his arms. "I'm here, baby. You're okay."

She wilted against him, and the wetness of her flesh and clothing dampened his chest. His heart crumpled, and he buried his face in the tangled locks of her hair.

"He's a monster," she whispered, her voice hoarse and broken.

"Who's a monster?"

"The man in the vision."

"He can't hurt you, baby. It was only an image."

Only a vision, but it was tearing her apart. It was pure anguish to watch her go through this, but nothing like the hell it must be for her. "Do you want to talk about it now or is it better to wait?"

"There's nothing to talk about. It was the nightmare all over again, only in more horrifying detail."

"The one with the green dress?"

She nodded and looked away.

"What were the new details, Dani? What changed?" He tilted her face toward him so that she'd have to make eye contact.

"Nothing important."

Her eyes said differently. "It wasn't Ella wearing the green dress, was it?"

"No," she admitted, "but it was a mistake. He thought I was someone named Helena. He thinks Ella or Helena or whatever her real name is betrayed him, that she took a lover."

"He said that."

"More than once. The killer has to be Kevin."

"Did you see his face?"

"No, but he's her boyfriend. Who else could she betray?"

"I'm not sure, but Ella being the victim's pseudo name fits with her using a fake social security number. What else was different?"

"The violence. The attack. He hit and..." Her

voice cracked. "There's no use to repeat it. He was just angry and violent and out for revenge."

"But you're sure the man thought he was harming someone else?"

"Yes, so as long as I don't put myself in a position to be confused with Ella, I should be safe."

She was trying to explain away the danger to herself the way she always did. He was convinced now that was for her benefit as much as his. If she believed she couldn't be touched by the reality of the violence, the visions couldn't destroy her.

Granted Marcus didn't know much about psychic visions, but he trusted his own gut instincts. He wasn't leaving her on her own until the man who'd already attacked Ella was locked behind bars.

He trailed his fingers down the smooth column of her neck to the collar of her pajamas. "You should get out of these wet clothes."

“These are the only pajamas I have with me.”

“If I owned a pair of pajamas, I’d lend you a top.” She’d probably surmised he didn’t since he was wearing only a pair of boxers now. “I can lend you one of my T-shirts. It’ll swallow you, but it should be comfortable enough.”

“That’ll work.”

“Good. I’ll get it. You just stay here and try to think calming, pleasant thoughts until I get back.” And not the kind of thoughts that had jumped into his mind at the image of her in one of his shirts. What was it with him that no matter how serious the situation, he couldn’t totally escape the chemistry between them?

She was in the bathroom when he returned. He heard the steady stream of water running in the basin and figured she was washing her face in the cold spray, trying to get her bearings again in the real world. Only with her, the nightmares had a way of becoming reality.

“Shirt’s hanging on the door,” he called.

"Thanks."

A nice dismissal. He should go back to his room now, walk away before he got a look at her draped in his shirt that would skim her body and hang to about mid-thigh. But he couldn't leave, not until he knew she was okay.

She opened the door a crack and grabbed the shirt. Seconds later she stepped out and trudged to the bed. She crawled in and pulled the covers to her waist. The shirt drooped, revealing one creamy shoulder.

"It's raining," she said. "I didn't realize that before."

"Yeah, it's been falling most of the night."

She rose to one elbow to plump her pillow. She was shivering when she finished and dropped her head again. "I wonder what goes on in a killer's mind on a dark, rainy night. Does he think about the upcoming kill? Does he imagine what it will feel like when he thrusts the dagger into a victim's heart?"

Oh, God. She was still trapped in the agony of the trance. He dropped to the edge of the bed. "We can talk a while if you like."

"I don't want to talk."

"I hate to leave you alone in this state."

"Then don't leave." She looked up and stared into his eyes. "Stay with me, Marcus. Please, just stay with me and hold me until I fall asleep."

It wasn't much to ask, unless she knew what it would take to stop at just holding her in his arms. But what kind of selfish bastard would say no to that request?

He crawled into bed beside her. Keeping his body on top of the covers, he slipped his left arm beneath her head.

She cuddled against him. "Thanks."

"Anytime." Any time at all or every night for the rest of his life.

He stiffened. What the hell was he thinking? And even more frightening, why did it feel so right?

THE TEMPERATURES HAD dropped to a cool fifty-one degrees by morning, but the sun had reappeared in all its glorious splendor. Dani had decided to go riding with Linney and the girls. Marcus had stayed behind. He'd used the time to check in with the local sheriff and see if he had new info regarding the attempted murder case.

He'd heard nothing but negatives. There were no prints on the dagger left in Ella's chest. The weapon was in the ancient Renaissance style, sold on the premises from two different vendors, and no record was kept of purchasers unless the customer used a credit card. Many didn't.

It had been verified that Kevin Flanders was in fact Ella's live-in boyfriend. He'd cooperated fully with the sheriff, insisting he wanted to get the dirty scum who was responsible.

His alibi for the time of the assault checked out, though it was far from ironclad. Supposedly he was playing cards and drinking beer with some male friends. Billy Germaine had vouched for him.

So much for Marcus's morning. He might as well have gone riding with the females. They were back at the house by eleven. After that, they'd eaten a quick lunch and left for Austin in Dani's car.

Marcus had left his truck at the ranch, figuring he could rent a car to get back to the Double M and drop it off in The Woodlands. He'd suggested Dani leave her car at the ranch and come back for it later. She'd balked at the idea, which in his mind meant she had no plans to return to Dobbin any time soon.

But apparently last night's trip to the outer realms had convinced her that Ella might not be the only one in danger. She hadn't put up any new arguments against his returning to Austin with her and taking enough luggage with him for a few nights' stay. As far as Celeste knew, he was merely coming to the area on a business trip and would be staying with them.

Marcus had taken over the driving chores. They were on the outskirts of Austin now, and traffic had practically come to a standstill. A guy behind him laid on his horn.

That'll do a lot of good, buddy.

"We're getting nowhere in this traffic jam," Dani said. "Take the next exit, and we'll stop by the nursing home and see my grandmother."

It was the first he'd heard of a grandmother. He worked his way into the exit lane, no easy task considering no one wanted to give an inch of freeway ground.

"Any special reason for the visit?"

"It's on the way," Dani said, "and Celeste hasn't seen her in a while."

"Good. I'd love to meet her." He suspected there was more to the visit than what Dani was willing to say in front of her daughter and Katie.

"I can't promise Grams will know any of us

are there," she said, "but occasionally she has lucid moments."

For Dani's sake, he hoped this would be one of those days, though he didn't know what she could say that would ease Dani's mind or shut off the visions.

Traffic came to a complete stop as they waited to exit. "This is almost as bad as Houston rush hour traffic."

Dani adjusted the flow of air from the air conditioner. "Life in the city."

"More reason to avoid them."

"We can't all live on the Double M."

True. That's why Texas was rich with ranches, many of them in the beautiful hill country all around them. He'd be thrilled even with a small one, land of his own and a roof with a spot beneath it to hang his Stetson. He'd get there some day.

"Visitor parking is in the side lot. You can drop the girls off at the door, and they can go to Grams's room and surprise her. I'll walk in with you."

Yep. She had her reasons for visiting Grams today, and he was about to hear about them, sans the two girls who'd been wired into their iPods for most of the trip.

He let them out and parked between a new Mercedes and a Porsche. Grandma's nursing home was most definitely not in the poverty zone.

He killed the engine. "Is this one of those talking moments?"

"It is," she said. "Grams is battling senility now, so her mind tends to wander into time's hinterlands more often than not. But when she was younger, her clairvoyant powers were legend."

So Grandma was a psychic, too. "Does Celeste know that?"

"No. Grams's powers diminished quickly after her first stroke. Celeste was only six at the time, so I was spared her learning the truth of her heritage."

"Have you ever thought of telling her? It's not as if it's something to be ashamed of."

"Don't go there with me, Marcus. You have no idea what you're talking about."

He'd pushed a button with that question, and this was not the time to rile Dani. "Is your mother also a psychic?"

"No. It's rare for the trait to be passed on. I'm praying I'm the only cursed offspring. Now, let's go in. If Grams seems cognizant today, I'd like a chance to talk to her alone. If she's totally out of it, there's no reason to bother. I'll take care of getting you out of the room if it comes to that."

"Your call," he said as they got out of the car and headed for the door.

The girls had gotten sidetracked by an elderly resident in the entry hall who wanted them to help her untangle a necklace that looked as if it had gotten caught in the spokes of a bicycle. They were all too glad to escape when Dani enlisted a volunteer to take over the task. An attendant greeted them and accompanied them down the hall.

Next stop, Grams. Another psychic, this one grappling with senility. Why did he think this couldn't be good?

Chapter Nine

Lucille Alevesta Alano sat in a wooden rocker in front of a window that looked out on an atrium. Songbirds flitted among the trees and fountains splashed in clear view of wheelchair-accessible walking paths.

A plaid shawl was draped over the woman's legs. Her blouse was almost the same shade of blue as the veins in her wrinkled face and hands. Her thin, white hair was neatly groomed but barely covered her scalp.

"Look who's here to see you," the smiling attendant announced. Lucille continued to stare out the window. "It's Dani and Celeste, and they've brought friends."

Still no response. Undaunted, Celeste hurried over and gave her grandmother a hug. "Hi, Grams. Guess what? I went horseback riding this morning and not at the stables. I was on a real ranch with cows and everything."

Ms. Alano smiled and scooted her chair around to face them, obviously not nearly as feeble as she looked. "I like horses." Her voice had a clatter in it, like an old car that needed to be tuned.

"Me, too, Grams. And we went to a Renaissance wedding. That's like from history, with knights and queens and ladies-in-waiting and all of that. Katie and I were fairies, but our wings got kind of bent."

"Dani was a beautiful bride."

"Yes, but this wasn't Dani's wedding, Grams. It was her friend Bethany Sue."

"You remember Bethany Sue," Dani said. "She used to come to our house when we lived in Louisiana."

"In Louisiana." Ms. Alano smiled. "We had flowers in the garden."

"Lots of flowers. Roses and peonies and night jasmine. And there was honeysuckle on the back fence."

"A magnolia tree."

"That's right, Grams. There was a huge magnolia tree in the front yard."

"Old Fred Dawson's dog got bitten by a copperhead," Ms. Alano added, her memory much better for things from long ago.

"That, I don't remember," Dani admitted. "But I remember that big black cur. He was always growling at me."

Dani pulled up a chair so that she sat right next to her grandmother. She took the old woman's frail right hand in both of hers. "This is my friend Marcus Abbot and Celeste's friend Katie."

The glazed look returned to Ms. Alano's eyes. "What did you say your name was?"

"I'm Dani, Grams. I'm your granddaughter."

"Dani." The woman nodded. "Do you want some candy? There's some in that bowl on my dresser."

The conversation went on like that for about ten minutes. Dani did most of the talking, and Celeste and Katie jumped in from time to time. If Dani had come here hoping for some kind of psychic epiphany concerning Ella, she was probably going to leave disappointed.

Dani turned to Marcus. Her eyes were creased with worry lines that he was almost certain hadn't been there two days ago. This was taking a toll on her.

"There's an ice cream shop on the next block, Marcus. Would you mind walking down there with the girls?"

Celeste sprang from the side of the bed where she'd been sitting. "Oh, yeah. Let's go there.

They have the best hot fudge sundae in the world—with mounds of whipped cream."

"Is that the place you told me about?" Katie asked. "The one where the fudge sauce tastes like real fudge?"

"Yeah, and they'll give you extra if you ask."

"You can pick up ice cream for Grams while you're there. She loves the chocolate mint. Just one small scoop in a cup."

So she'd decided to try to get through to her grandmother. He'd take the bait and leave her alone for a few minutes. If he didn't she might lock him out of the town house.

"We can go by ourselves if you don't want to go," Celeste offered.

"And miss out on the best hot fudge sundae in the world with extra topping? No way!"

Dani reached for her purse.

"I'll spring for the ice cream," he assured her. "Anything for you?"

"A Diet Coke with lots of ice."

No wonder she stayed so thin and fit into that slim pencil skirt and buttery soft sweater so well. All chic, all the time. Definitely a sophisticated, city woman.

Bear that in mind if you ever start to think you have a real chance with her, cowboy.

"I have my cell phone," he said. "Call if you change your mind about the ice cream or if you need anything at all."

"Ice cream," Grams said. "Chocolate mint."

Dani only nodded.

DANI KNEW HER GRANDMOTHER'S mental limitations. She was approaching her ninety-sixth birthday, and senility had set in with a vengeance. She regretted now the years she'd lost with her, years when Dani had tried to escape her psychic background by avoiding contact with the woman who had bequeathed her the dubious gift.

Fortunately, she'd reconnected with Grams

a few years back and had been there for her when she'd had her first stroke. From that point on, her psychic abilities had dimmed. If she had visions these days, the staff mistook them for side effects of her many medications. Dani wasn't convinced that Grams had lost all her powers.

She waited until she was sure Marcus and the girls were out of hearing range. Dropping to her knees in front of Grams, she positioned herself where she was at eye level with her. "I've been having visions, Grams. Very frightening visions."

Grams said nothing, but she didn't look away. Dani took that as a good sign. She didn't want to frighten her grandmother, but she'd always had such strong insights into apparitions and the paranormal. And Dani desperately needed guidance now, for her sake and Ella's.

"I keep seeing this woman in a green

Elizabethan ball gown. Someone is trying to stab her with a dagger."

Still no response. "A woman was stabbed the night of the wedding. She looks almost just like me, Grams. A woman about my age who looks so much like me, people could get us confused. We could be twins."

"Twins. Baby no-name."

"She's not a baby, Grams. She's my age. She has a name, maybe two names. Ella and Helena. She sells Renaissance-styled clothing."

"Baby no-name. You found her?"

"No, not a baby. A woman, like me."

Grams squirmed and rubbed her hands together, seeming to grow more alert. "Your mother couldn't help what she did. She was young, and we were poor. No men to help us. No one to take care of the farm."

Grams had drifted back into her past. If Dani persisted in trying to reach her, it would frustrate both of them. "Let's take a walk through the atrium, Grams. A little exercise will do us both good."

Talk of baby no-name and tales of Grams's ancient past definitely wouldn't.

MARCUS FOUND DANI and her grandmother in the atrium. He knew from the look on Dani's face that she'd gotten nowhere. No surprise there. He handed Dani the cola and the ice cream. "Your grandmother had better eat this quickly," he said. "It's already starting to melt."

"I'll get her a real spoon from the kitchen," Dani said. "She hates the plastic ones." She hurried off and left him with Ms. Alano.

Marcus shifted from one boot to the other. He was never all that comfortable with elderly women. He could talk war, sports, daily news and livestock. That never seemed to fascinate them.

"Young man."

Something about him had captured her attention. His being here might have upset her. Her voice sounded different than it had earlier. It still clattered, but the speech was more distinct.

"You're Dani's man."

That was pushing things a bit. "Dani and I are friends."

"The man with the dagger…"

"What about him?"

"Save her."

Marcus stepped closer. "Save her from whom, Ms. Alano? Who has the dagger?"

"Her man."

"Whose man? Dani's? Ella Somerville's?"

"No-name baby. Poor little thing."

Marcus muttered a few curses under his breath. If she'd been there at all, he was losing her. "Who wants Dani dead?"

"Her man. He's evil. Have to save Dani."

"Ms. Alano. I have to know more if I'm

going to protect Dani. Who wants to kill her? I need his name so I can stop him."

She stared into space as if she hadn't heard him. "I want to go to my room. I want to watch TV."

"In a minute. First tell me who wants to kill Dani."

She pointed at the cup of ice cream Dani had left sitting on the bench. "Is that chocolate mint?"

"Yes. Dani went to get you a spoon. Think, Ms. Alano. Who wants Dani dead?"

"Hand me that ice cream, young man."

He'd lost her. Exasperation weighed like a bag of cement on his chest.

Dani returned with the spoon. Her grandmother looked at her and smiled. "What's your name, dear?"

They were back to square one. This psychic world was really starting to get on his nerves. He didn't know if Ms. Alano had envisioned a killer or if she was repeating a confused version of something Dani had said to her while he was buying ice cream.

Save Dani.

He planned to, with or without the ambiguous visions and psychic mumbo jumbo. He'd do this his way, the SEAL way where success was the only option.

MARCUS TOOK THE KEY and opened the door to Dani's posh town house, checking for any sign that it had been broken into, before he stepped aside for her and Celeste to enter.

"Nice pad," he said, eyeing the crystal chandelier and the art hung above the antique chest in the marble foyer. "Duran Muton must like you a lot."

"Not this much. I divorced well."

More surprises. He really knew very little about the woman who now completely consumed his hours and thoughts. "Good thing

I didn't drive here in my truck. Your neighbors would have had it towed."

"Nonsense. They'd have taken you for a repairman," she teased. "The guest suite is on the third level, but you can just leave your luggage by the stairs until you're ready to go up."

"Guest *suite?*"

"No biggie. It's a family-size town house and there are only two of us."

"But no room for horses," Celeste said, frowning. "I'm going to e-mail my friends and tell them all about our trip." She pranced up to the second floor, taking the wide steps two at a time.

Dani slipped out of her jacket. "Give me a minute to check my phone messages, and I'll give you a tour of the place. In the meantime, just make yourself at home."

Sure he'd make himself at home, about as home as he'd feel in the Taj Mahal. One wrong move and he'd surely break something, like that delicate porcelain statue on the shelf near his elbow. Three ballerinas, all on their toes. There was a silver-framed picture of Celeste and Dani on the antique foyer table that he admired from a safe distance. He tried that for a few seconds, then took his chances and ventured into the high-ceilinged living area.

The furnishings were Hollywood or something from the cover of a decorating magazine. He'd never realized normal people actually lived like this—or how they lived like this.

Case in point, the overstuffed sofa was upholstered in white. Who'd ever trust a guy to watch football and eat chips on a white sofa?

The coffee table was polished to a high shine and topped with a crystal bowl filled with colored glass balls and blooming orchids. Even with his boots off, he didn't see a spot for his feet. And if there was a television in the room, it was well hidden.

The kitchen was more like it. Still fancy, but at least it had the basic instruments for survival—once you located and identified them. The refrigerator was built into the cabinets with the same beautiful wood on the front.

The range was the latest design, and the coffeepot looked like a contraption from a Star Wars control center. He might not have known what it was had the word *espresso* not been engraved into the chrome.

"No messages of importance," Dani said, joining him in the kitchen. "What do you think of the place so far?"

"It suits you."

"That doesn't particularly sound like a compliment."

"It's a nice place."

"But?"

He wasn't doing this well. The problem was that he was trying to see himself in this setting, and it didn't fly. But his presence was only temporary here and in Dani's world. "I'm used to ranch life," he said, "and Navy bunks. This is a little rich for my blood."

"For mine, as well. Todd and I bought and furnished the town house together when he closed the deal on his first big contract. He has a flair for the dramatic and putting on the dog. I'd have gone for a bit more coziness. Celeste and I have made enough changes that we're comfortable here."

"That must have been a nice contract. What kind of work does your ex do?"

"Todd invented a device used in drilling operations. I don't understand the complexities of it fully, but according to Todd it's now a staple in the oil and gas industry."

"Did he come up with that while you were married?"

"He did, which meant he had to give up the house, furnishings, my car—all three paid for in full—and a nice chunk of change in order to bed and wed his new love interest. Apparently he felt it was worth that to get rid of me."

The guy might be a genius on some front, but he had to be nuts to give up Dani. "So if you have all this money, why do you work?"

"The chunk is not that big. I love my job. Tennis and hanging out at the country club bore me. Two martini lunches with the rich-bitch set give me headaches. All of the above."

"I hear that." He opened the back door and looked out. There was a flagstone patio, nicely furnished with teak tables, cushioned chairs and a built-in grill. A few square yards of manicured garden space stretched between that and a privacy fence. Beyond that were more town houses with not a tree in sight.

"I know this must feel suffocating to you," Dani said, obviously reading his mind. "But it's near my work and Celeste's private girls' school. It's perfect for us."

"That's all that matters."

One hand slid to rest on her shapely hip. "This is how people live in the city, Marcus. I don't need acres of lawn to keep up."

"No use to go to the defensive. I said it's nice. Besides, I'm just a guest."

She sighed. "Stay outside as long as you like. I'm going to call the hospital and check on Ella. I'm starting to get really bad vibes about her."

And probably worse vibes about him.

In Ella's case, he wasn't sure if vibes meant psychic mind grumblings or something more subtle, but nothing about Ella Somerville's situation made him feel good.

He followed Dani back inside. He started upstairs to take his luggage and survey his *suite* when the panic in Dani's voice stopped him cold. His gut tightened. The saga of Ella Somerville had apparently taken a turn for the worse.

DREAD CHOKED DANI'S WORDS. "There must be some mistake. I called earlier today and a nurse said Ella had been moved to a semiprivate room, but that she was still in serious condition."

"She was moved to room 506 this morning. Are you a relative?"

Dani decided on a lie. A no might get her a curt "I'm sorry we can't release any more information." "I'm her sister."

"Then hopefully you can persuade her to return to the hospital at once."

"Then she wasn't discharged?"

"Hardly. She sneaked from the floor after stealing a robe from the closet of the other patient in her room."

"What time was that?"

"A little over an hour ago, sometime between three-thirty and four-thirty. Kevin Flanders came to visit. He brought a beautiful bouquet of roses. When he went in to give it to her, her bed was empty."

"Maybe she just wandered off and got lost. It's a big hospital."

"We've searched the premises. She's gone and so is her handbag. Can you hold on a moment? Dr. Carson's walking this way right now. I'm sure he'd like to speak to you. Can I have your name?"

"Dani," she said, avoiding her last name. "I'll hold."

Her irritation heightened to match her sky-rocketing anxiety. All of this had transpired within the past hour, and her psychic abilities had been worthless. They'd provided no inkling as to where Ella had gone, no clue if she'd left the hospital on her own or had been abducted.

What is it you want from me? How can I help if all you let me see is bits and pieces and never the whole thing? Show me the villain!

"Dr. Carson is ready to speak to you."

"I'm still here."

"Hello." The deep male voice resonated with authority. "Am I speaking to Ella's sister?"

"Yes." The lie was starting to come too easily.

"Are you aware that she walked out of the hospital today without being medically released?"

"I wasn't until I called the hospital a few minutes ago."

"Well, she did, and our hands are tied when patients make that decision on their own. Do you know where she is or how to reach her?"

No, and if that wasn't bad enough, the man who'd tried to kill her might try again. "I'll try to locate her," Dani said. "Did Ella say anything to anyone about where she was going, perhaps her roommate?"

"No, and no one saw her walk past the nurses' desk. There's an emergency staircase just outside her room. She may have left that way."

Unless she was abducted and carried down the stairs. But Dani couldn't imagine an abductor stealing a robe.

"Ella's in critical condition," the doctor stressed. "We can't force medical care on her, but if you have any influence with her, I suggest you see that she gets it, either here or at some other medical facility."

"I'll see what I can do."

"Good. For her sake, I hope you're successful. Patients who've been through a trauma don't always understand the risk they're taking by refusing care." To his credit, his voice took on a tone of real concern.

"I'll find a way to get her back to a hospital," she assured him, though she wasn't sure how she was going to accomplish the task.

Her insides rolled, and a wave of vertigo sent her head spinning. When it passed, she spotted Marcus on the landing, watching her, his worn duffel in hand.

"Don't bother to unpack. There's been a change of plans."

Chapter Ten

Once Dani made up her mind, there was no changing it. As much as Marcus didn't like being cooped up in a town house on a postage-stamp lot, he preferred it to Dani's playing Good Samaritan.

Nonetheless, a couple of phone calls and Dani had been ready to head back to Dobbin. She'd arranged for a caretaker to come for Celeste, the same lady who regularly stayed with her when Dani was out of town on business. She'd asked for and gotten approval for up to five vacation days, if needed.

And they were off.

It was fifteen minutes past nine o'clock in the evening by the time they reached the town limits for Plantersville.

"I still don't see the point of you taking this on yourself," Marcus said. "What ever happened to hiring protection for Ella?"

"I told you. No one I hire will have my psychic abilities, which means I have the best chance of locating her."

"And the first place you want to look for her is at her travel trailer."

"It makes sense, Marcus. It's her home. She may feel safest there with Kevin Flanders to protect and take care of her."

"In which case you'd think he'd take her back to the hospital where she belongs."

"Maybe he tried and she wouldn't go."

"If she won't go for him, what makes you think she'll go for you?"

"I can promise her protection. If she knows

there's an armed guard at her door 24/7, that she's safer in the hospital than anywhere else, then it makes sense for her to go back and get the treatment she needs."

"Have you forgotten what she told you last night?"

"No. Look, I don't expect you to understand, but I have to give this a try. Even if she's not at the RV, I may see or feel something that triggers a new trance, one that will lead me to her."

Marcus admired Dani's tenacity and her determination to protect a virtual stranger. He loathed that she had to get in the middle of everything herself. It wasn't smart, not when all she had to go on was vague visions that put her in as much danger as Ella—maybe more.

Still he turned at the highway that led to the festival grounds. He didn't fully understand how these telepathic connections worked. Maybe Dani would handle one of Ella's possessions and pick up a psychic scent, kind of like a good bomb dog could sniff out explosives.

That didn't mean he had to like Dani's involvement in any of this.

Only one thing stopped him from putting his foot down and insisting she hire a private investigator to search for Ella. Well, two things. One, she'd probably step right over his foot.

Two, he figured getting the truth from Ella was the best way to find out why the visions kept showing Dani at the point of a dagger.

WHEN SHE'D PASSED the festival campgrounds on Saturday, Dani noticed trailers scattered about the clearing a few yards off the road.

Saturday. Only two days ago. It seemed weeks. Dani was used to busy days, but never had she crammed this much into forty-eight hours.

Lights flickered off to her left, and then the silhouettes of tents began to form in the darkness. Dani sat completely still, hoping for some psychic sensation that she was on the right track.

Marcus slowed the car. “We’re close. Getting any vibrations?”

“Nothing,” she admitted.

“That makes two of us. But remember your promise.”

“Right, commando.” She tipped her head saucily. “I follow your lead and don’t go anywhere without you. And no back talk.”

She’d added the last part on her own. He reached across the back of her seat and gave her shoulder a reassuring squeeze. She struggled to ignore the sensual urge the insignificant touch induced. She’d have enough trouble dealing with those later, when she was sleeping a few steps away from him.

This could be a very long night.

“I’M LOOKING FOR ELLA Somerville. She owns one of the clothing shops inside the festival. Do you know her?”

The dark-haired woman stood in the door of her small travel trailer, holding a sandwich in one hand and a beer in the other. "I don't think so. A group of people who work here have camps set up toward the back of the grounds. Did you check there?"

"Not yet." But she definitely would now. "Thanks for your help."

A mosquito buzzed in Dani's ear. She swatted it away and walked back to the truck with Marcus. He'd been patient beyond measure, and quieter than he'd been since she'd met him. She suspected he was sorry he'd ever handed her his card.

He drove to the back of the grounds. There were several travel trailers, most with lights on. Someone had strung up a clothesline outside one and there were two skirts billowing in the breeze. A preschool boy kicked a soccer ball outside another.

"Eenie, meanie, miney, moe," Marcus said.

"Let's try the one with laundry still hanging."

"You got it."

Dani parked and Marcus walked her to the door. She knew he had his weapon on him, ready for any kind of trouble. It shocked her how literally he took her psychic visions. Even from the beginning, Todd had hated any mention of them and belittled her for believing they existed.

Marcus knocked and stayed between her and the door until a very attractive woman who looked to be in her early twenties opened it. She was wearing nothing but talcum and a sheer nightshirt.

The near nude smiled broadly. "Well, hello, cowboy."

Shameless flirt, but who could blame her. Hunks like Marcus didn't come knocking every night. At least they hadn't at Dani's door.

"Down, boy," Dani whispered, stepping closer. "We're looking for someone who's camping in the area. Ella Somerville. Do you know her?"

"Yeah, sure. She and Kevin live in that blue

and white trailer where the Jeep and the Honda Civic are parked. You know you look almost just like Ella. You must be kin."

"Sisters."

"Then I guess you heard what happened to her the other night. I couldn't believe it. We never have any trouble around here. I mean never. We don't even lock up, unless we're going to be gone overnight. And now Ella gets stabbed while working a private wedding party. It's bizarre. How is she anyway?"

"Critical."

"Oh, no."

To the woman's credit, she looked genuinely upset.

"Have you heard any speculation as to who might have stabbed her?" Marcus asked.

"No. I heard the police questioned Kevin, but I can't believe he'd try to kill her. I mean, he's a loudmouth, especially when he's high—or drunk. Not the type to commit murder, though. I guess people always say that about someone they know, don't they?"

"Not always," Marcus answered. "Thanks for your help."

"Anytime. And if you're ever in the neighborhood, stop in."

"Can't get a more forthright invitation than that, cowboy." Dani mocked the woman's flirty tone as they walked back to the car.

"Lady's just being friendly."

"*Lady's* not the word I'd have chosen."

He opened the passenger door for her and leaned in close. "You're not jealous, are you?"

"Me. Not a chance," she lied and smiled sweetly.

"I didn't think so."

His tone was teasing, but neither the spark of jealousy nor the banter eased Dani's apprehension as they approached the door to the blue and white trailer. It was old, a bit battered, but one of the larger ones around. The sides had been extended to provide extra living space. There were lights on inside and voices.

Marcus rapped on the metal door. Dani sucked in a ragged breath, and all of a sudden she reeled from an aura of all-encompassing evil. It whirled around the muscular body of the man who'd answered the door.

He looked familiar, but it took a few minutes to place him as one of the jousters. He was barefoot in spite of the cooler night-time temperatures and wearing a stained gray T-shirt and a pair of denim jeans with frayed holes.

"Kevin Flanders?" Marcus asked.

"Yeah." Kevin rattled the keys in his pocket and shifted nervously, staring at Dani as if he were seeing Ella's ghost.

"We're looking for Ella Somerville," Marcus said. "Is she here?"

"Who wants to know?"

"My name's Marcus Abbot."

"And the woman?"

"She's with me." Marcus's tone and the strain to his muscles made it clear that was all Kevin needed to know. "Now, about Ella?"

Kevin hooked his thumbs through his empty belt loops. "Are you cops?"

"A private investigator."

Marcus pulled a leather tri-fold from his front pocket and flashed his ID. Dani had forgotten he was official, not carrying any authority, but official.

Kevin barely glanced at the card, but he eyed both her and Marcus suspiciously. "Ella's not home. She was attacked and stabbed Saturday night, but I'm guessing you already know that." He scratched the back of his right leg with the big toe of his left foot while he studied them. "Did the hospital send you?"

"The attending doctor is concerned about Ella's leaving the hospital in her condition,"

Marcus said, sidestepping the question. "He feels her health is in jeopardy unless she returns at once."

"I don't know what I can do about that. She's not here. I keep thinking she'll show up, but she hasn't even called. I don't know if she's scared or what. She gets funny ideas at times. I called the cops and told them she was missing. They said they'll look into it."

He opened the door wider. "You wanna come in?"

Dani most definitely did, and she wasn't leaving until she knew for certain Ella wasn't inside. She pushed past Kevin. Another man was sitting on the couch, his shirt littered with peanuts that had apparently missed his mouth. He brushed them off and stood when she entered.

"This here's Billy Germaine," Kevin said. "He's a friend, a jouster, same as me."

Billy extended his hand to Marcus but only

stared at Dani. The similarity between her and Ella was apparently freaking him out, too.

"The hospital sent them," Kevin informed Billy as he picked up a handful of empty beer cans from the coffee table and tossed them into a large white plastic trash can a few steps away. "They're looking for Ella."

Billy glared at Marcus. "You look like a cop to me."

"Would it matter if I was? Kevin here tells me he'd welcome police involvement in locating Ella."

"The only involvement they want is to try to pin the stabbing on Kevin."

"Knock it off, Billy," Kevin ordered. "The deputies questioned me, that's all."

"Only reason they didn't arrest you is because you have an alibi. They always try to pin the crime on the boyfriend. Everybody knows that."

"I'm not a cop," Marcus said.

"Does Ella have any friends or family in the

area, someone she might have gone to stay with?" Dani asked. She kept her tone even, hoping to break the tension.

"No friends in Texas that I know of," Kevin said. "No family at all, at least none that she'll admit to having."

"I heard you have visited her at the hospital," Dani said. "Did she tell you anything about her attacker?"

"She wasn't saying anything to anybody while I was there last night. Then when I went back this afternoon, she was gone."

"There was an eyewitness to the stabbing," Billy offered. "The officers who questioned Kev said she told them the perp was wearing full..."

"Wait a minute," Kevin interrupted. He pointed a finger at Dani. "You're the eyewitness, aren't you?"

"Why would you think that?"

"One of the deputies mentioned that she

looked a lot like Ella. That has to be you. They said you might have been the intended victim."

"I don't know if I was supposed to be the victim or not, but I am the only eyewitness," Dani admitted. "The important thing right now is finding Ella and getting her back to the hospital."

Her head started to spin. The force of evil inside the trailer was overpowering.

"Are you okay?" Marcus asked, obviously sensing her distress.

"I'm feeling a bit nauseated. I think it's that spicy food we had for dinner." Marcus would know they hadn't eaten yet and would get the message. Kevin and Billy wouldn't. She looked to Kevin. "May I use your bathroom?"

"Sure, down the hall. You can't miss it. Don't trip over that pile of old newspapers. Trash builds up fast in a small RV like this one."

She stepped over the newspapers, noting the headlines. "Hurricane Preparedness Costs

Rising." The *Pensacola News Journal.* She purposely tripped just enough to scatter the stack. At least one more of the newspapers was also the *Pensacola News Journal.* She didn't see Kevin as a reader, but maybe Pensacola was home to Ella.

She paused at the bathroom door and glanced behind her. Marcus could see her from where he was standing. The others couldn't. She walked past the bathroom and opened the only other door inside the trailer. Light from the hallway spilled onto the bed.

She exhaled quickly, releasing the breath she'd been holding in dread. Her fears hadn't materialized. Ella wasn't gagged and tied to the bedposts. Her dead body wasn't sprawled across the sheets.

Closing the door behind her, Dani flicked on the overhead light. The bed was unmade, and a pair of Kevin's wrinkled jeans and a T-shirt lay on the floor near the closet. Tiptoeing to the built-in chest, she eased open the top drawer, cringing when it squeaked.

Ella's intimates were stacked neatly—bras, panties and a pair of silk pantaloons. Dana held up the pantaloons and crushed them to her chest. The evil in the house still clogged her lungs, but that was it. Nothing was elicited from Ella's clothing.

The closet door was open. She walked over and stared at the contents. It was extremely neat with a clear divide. About two thirds of the closet was filled with period dresses, skirts and blouses, most likely from Ella's shop. The other third was jeans, shirts and two cocktail dresses. One red. One black. Boots and shoes lined the shelf above the hangers. Sandals and tennis shoes stood in a neat row on the floor. A crate holding stuffed manila folders sat in one corner.

Nothing in the closet belonged to Kevin—unless it was the files. Apparently he had his own space somewhere else in the trailer, or maybe all of his things were stuffed into drawers.

Dani searched the rack of Renaissance dresses. Her heart slammed against her chest as her focus settled on an all-too-familiar ball gown. Jade velvet. It was exactly like the one she'd seen in the shop that first day, a replica of the one that Ella had been wearing when she was stabbed.

Apparently, Ella liked it so well that she'd kept two for herself. Not so unusual, she decided, since there were a half-dozen skirts and peasant blouses in the same style.

The knight. The dagger. The dress. All from Ella's life—not hers.

Dani pulled the dress from the closet and held it up in front of her, staring at her reflection in the full-length mirror on the closet door. A damp fog crept into the room. Death. It was all around her. She smelled the fear. Tasted the horror.

The stench of the dress became stifling, but

she couldn't put it down. Her knees went weak, and the fog seeped through her skull and took over her mind.

"Put on the dress."

"No, please."

"Put on the dress for me. Wear it for me the way you wore it for him."

"I never..."

The door flew open. Kevin was standing there, his face red and explosive. Vile curses flew from his mouth, and his fingers dug into the flesh of her upper arm as he yanked the gown from her hands.

"Take your hands off her. *Now,*" Marcus ordered, stepping into the crowded bedroom with Billy following on his heels.

"Don't order me around," Kevin snapped. "This is my house, and you're not a cop." His grip tightened on her arm.

"Right. I'm not a cop. I don't have rules. Now take your hands off her, or I'll tear your arms out of the sockets and hand them to you like kindling."

Marcus was livid, his muscles hard and flexed, the veins in his neck and face distended. She'd never seen him like this, a missile ready to detonate. She had to do something to diffuse the situation before it got totally out of hand.

"I'm okay, Marcus. Let's just…"

It was all she got out before Billy grabbed Marcus's arms from behind and pinned them behind his back. "Teach him a lesson, Kev. Give him what he deserves."

Marcus's jaw jutted at a defiant angle. "I wouldn't advise it, Kev."

"What are you going to do about it, cowboy?" Kevin released his grip on her and doubled his fist, yanking it back before plowing it into Marcus's stomach. Not once, but twice. Sweat popped out on Marcus's brow.

Dani dived for the lamp to break it over

Kevin's head. Kevin pulled off Marcus and wrenched the lamp from her hands. He shoved her against the closet door. Her head banged against the wooden frame.

Marcus erupted into a fighting machine. His right foot connected with Kevin's chest, sending the man stumbling backward. In a lightning-fast move, the back of Marcus's head crashed into Billy's face. Blood from Billy's nose splattered Marcus's hair and shoulders.

Billy lost his grip on Marcus, and before he could get in a blow, Marcus threw a punch that sent him careening against the bedpost. He held on to it and slowly slid to the floor.

Kevin came up with a baseball bat he'd grabbed from under the bed. Dani jumped on his back and tried to lock her arms around his neck. He elbowed her in the ribs and shook her off, just as Ella's attacker had done Saturday night.

He swung the bat at Marcus's head. Marcus dodged it and planted a succession of blows to

Kevin's upper body and jaw. Kevin slumped to the floor. Marcus clenched the fabric at the neck of Kevin's T-shirt and pulled him back to a standing position.

Kevin muttered a string of curses and groaned in pain. "You're nuts, man. Look at Billy. I think you broke his jaw."

"Want to go two for the price of one?"

"Just get out of my house."

"Glad to oblige as soon as the lady gets an apology."

"Yeah, I'm sorry," Kevin mumbled insincerely, never looking up.

That was more than enough for Dani. "Let's just go," she said.

Marcus wrapped an arm around her shoulder. "Are you sure you're okay?"

She nodded and Marcus led her to the kitchen, opened the freezer compartment and took out a few cubes of ice. He tore a handful of paper towels from a half-empty roll and wrapped them around the ice. "Put this on that bump on your head."

"Thanks." Her head throbbed, but she'd fared a lot better than Billy and Kevin. "You should come with a warning label that classifies you as a deadly weapon."

"I do." He fingered the chain around his neck and the SEAL trident pendant he wore like a talisman. "Never mess with a frogman."

Call her crazy, but at this minute she'd never wanted to tangle with anyone more.

DANI STEPPED INTO the hot bath. Only her third night in Marcus's rustic cabin and it already had a surprising familiarity about it. A casual late dinner of BLT sandwiches and smooth red wine at his marred wooden table had felt positively cozy, except for the conversation about Kevin's black aura of evil.

She was convinced now that he was Ella's attacker. Marcus hadn't argued with that assessment, nor had he agreed with it. He wanted facts. So would the deputies.

She sank beneath the hot water and the layer of fragrant bubbles. She'd brought the bubble bar from home, as well as her new champagne-colored silk pajamas and a matching robe. Not too sexy or revealing, but feminine, and the color brought out her eyes and the sun-lightened highlights in her hair.

Last night she'd fallen asleep in Marcus's arms. No real intimacy, no seductive touch, no kiss. That was probably for the best. The nightmare had left her a nervous wreck, and she wasn't sure passion would have mixed well with that.

Ever since their kiss, she'd struggled to keep the desire he ignited under control. The need was stronger than ever tonight. She'd seen a different side of him in Ella's trailer. He'd looked and acted like a Greek war god, all muscle and strength and masculinity.

But he hadn't used excessive force. He didn't beat them to a pulp, though it was clear he could have. He just took care of business more impressively than any movie superhero she'd ever seen.

The manners of a cowboy. The fighting soul of an American serviceman and protector. She'd never been so turned on.

Call it chemistry. Call it infatuation. Call it lust. Call it anything you wanted. All she knew was that she ached to feel his lips on hers again. Hungered for the taste of him and the thrill when their breaths mingled and her body fit so close to his she could feel his passion swelling between them.

He'd wanted her the other day by the river. She was sure of it. So why was he keeping her at a distance now? Was it something she'd done, or were her psychic lapses such a turnoff for him that it killed his desire for her? Even Todd hadn't come to detest them this quickly.

Whatever it was, she needed to know. She'd never been one to beat around the bush. When the bubbles melted, she'd go to his bedroom and insist on the truth.

THE LIGHT WAS ON in the kitchen when Dani went to look for Marcus. She found him at the pine table with his laptop and some scribbled notes. His hair was still damp from the shower. His shirt was off, revealing a couple of nasty scratches stretching across his left shoulder and a developing bruise just under his chin.

"How's your head?" he asked, without looking up.

"The goose egg is still there, but it doesn't hurt anymore."

"Headache? Nausea?"

"Neither. I'm sure I don't have a concussion," she assured him for the second time that night. "You need some antibiotic ointment on those scratches."

"They're nothing. I just got some news from the sheriff's office. A car was reported stolen from the parking lot of the hospital during the same time period that Ella went missing. A woman left her keys in the ignition while she ran in to drop off a payment envelope in the business office."

"Ella must have taken her car."

"That's a distinct possibility."

"That's good news, isn't it? An abductor would have surely brought his own getaway vehicle. And if Ella took the car, all we have to do is find it and we have her."

"The car hasn't been located yet."

"Surely finding it is a top priority."

Marcus double-clicked, and a new page started loading on his laptop. "Finding stolen cars are never a top priority unless there's an armed crime involved."

"Not even when the woman who stole it needs medical attention?"

"Indicators are that Ella left the hospital of her own free will. I'm not saying the authorities aren't trying to locate her, but don't expect miracles."

"Still, how far can she go dressed in a robe?"

"The owner of the car was on her way to Macy's to return a purchase. She had a bag with a pair of jeans and two sweaters in the backseat. The jeans were a size ten. The sweaters were size small. I'm guessing those would fit Ella."

"The sweaters would. The jeans might be baggy on her, but she could wear them." A choking knot formed in Dani's chest. She went to the sink, filled a glass full of cool water and drank it slowly.

"We'll find her, Dani—but then what? You can't force her to go back to the hospital any more than you can force her to accept a bodyguard. I'm not sure how you see this playing out."

"I see her safe and fully recovered from the

stabbing. I see her selling her beautiful Renaissance clothing to countless women in dozens of towns. And I see Kevin Flanders in jail."

Her words sounded good, but the assumptions were gross exaggerations. She didn't see anything but the images the spirits from the outer realms allowed her to see. She saw death and evil and blood on a jade velvet gown. But why pull her into Ella's life at all if the visions weren't meant to help save her?

One of the scratches on Marcus's back oozed a few drops of blood. Dani went to his bathroom and rummaged though the cabinets until she found his first-aid supplies. He'd protest, but she'd tend to his wounds anyway. He'd have done the same for her.

He was still poring over the monitor when she returned. "What's so interesting?" she asked as she unscrewed the cap on the small bottle of peroxide.

"Daggers. I'm checking to see how many sites I can pull up that sell weapons similar to the one used in the attack."

"The sheriff said you could buy them at the festival, so why would you think the culprit would go online?"

"To keep the seller from recognizing him and reporting the purchase to the police."

"You mean if the attacker happened to be someone well-known around the festival—like Kevin Flanders."

"His name comes to mind."

"What did you find?"

"That sites that sell daggers from that maker are plentiful. It would take weeks to check all the dealers' records, especially if the sellers insisted on search warrants."

Dani wet a gauze pad with the peroxide and dabbed the liquid on the deeper scratch.

Marcus winced. "What was that?"

"Relax, tough guy. All you'll feel is a sting,

if that." She squeezed a thin ribbon of the antibiotic cream onto her fingertips. Bracing herself with a hand on his strong right shoulder, she applied the cream with smooth, gentle strokes.

A slow burn started at her fingertips and spread to her chest, working its way to her inner thighs. Passion vibrated through her until she could almost feel a curl of invisible steam rising between them.

Marcus reached behind him and took her hand and moved it away. "That's good enough."

She couldn't let this go on any longer.

"I thought you were as into the kiss we shared by the river as much as I was, Marcus, but now you avoid my touch as if I'm contagious with some rare, fatal disease."

"It's not that bad."

"It's close. Is it something I've done?"

"No, of course not." He stood and walked to

the counter, leaning against it to face her from a distance.

"Then what is it? Why can't you stand my touch?"

"It's just the opposite, Dani. Everything you do makes me crazier for you. I'm like a sailor who hasn't had leave in years."

"Then why pull away from me the way you did just now?"

He ran his fingers through his damp hair. "Because if I don't pull away, I'm going to take you into my arms and make love with you like there's no tomorrow. That's not fair to you in your vulnerable state, and it would be murder on my concentration when I need to think about nothing but keeping you safe."

She walked toward him, stopping so near they were almost touching. "What about what I want, Marcus? Don't I have a say in any of this?"

"No."

"That's not fair." She massaged the muscles in his broad shoulders, then let her hands slip to his chest to explore the carpet of coppery hairs. "I'm not asking for forever, Marcus. I'm asking for tonight. I don't know if it's the danger, the tumultuous visions or if it's just you, but I've never felt this way with anyone else. I've never needed anyone the way I need you, not once in all my life."

She slid her fingers lower, trailing the area where the vee of hair tapered off and disappeared inside his jeans.

He moaned softly and splayed his hands across her back. "You're driving me completely mad with wanting you, Dani. If you're not sure this is what you want, you need to back off now."

"I'm sure I want you, Marcus. In my arms. In my bed. Inside me."

He groaned and swept her into his arms. "You win, sweetheart, hands down. I can face an enemy eight nights a week, but I'm not nearly tough enough to say no to an offer like that from you."

Chapter Eleven

Every moment since Marcus had first spotted Dani at the festival had been moving them toward this moment. The attraction had been immediate and dynamic, as if something inside him had short-circuited.

He wasn't the kind of guy to believe in Hollywood-type serendipity. Hell, he probably couldn't even spell the word. Sure, he knew about fate from a frogman's point of view. Knew how a man could escape a bullet or an explosion by a matter of seconds. Knew the thin line between landing in the ocean or on a land mine that wasn't twenty feet away.

But having a woman you barely knew rock your soul with passion—that was out there, miles beyond any frame of reference he had. Something had happened when he met Dani. He'd wanted her in every way, and the thought of making love with her was total intoxication.

He carried her down the hall and kicked open the door to her room. He ached to kiss her sweet lips, but once he started, it would be eons before he'd come up for air. Better make it to the bed first. He yanked back the quilt and laid her on top of the crisp, white sheets.

She smiled and opened her arms to him. He fell to the bed beside her and pulled her against him, finally touching his lips to hers. She melted into the kiss, and the thrill rocked through him. No holds barred now.

He wanted it all. Planned to kiss every inch

of her silky flesh, find the special spots that made her writhe in pleasure. Would delve into the hot triangle between her thighs until she was moist and so ready that she begged him to push inside her and rock her home.

The problem was his own body was so on fire he didn't know how long he could last.

When Dani pulled out of the kiss, his lungs were burning. He leaned away so that he could see the full length of her stretched out beside him. He kissed the curve in her neck. "You have on way too many clothes for a lady begging to be seduced."

"I figured a highly trained man like yourself would know how to remedy that."

He pushed the silky robe from her shoulders, and she wiggled her arms out of the sleeves. With that done, he tugged it away and dropped it to the floor.

Now he could see her perky breasts pushed against the fabric of her pajamas, the nipples peaked and pointing right at him. Enticing. Inviting.

He loosened the buttons slowly, trailing kisses along the way as her top fell open.

Finally, he added it to the growing pile of discarded silk. He cupped her right breast in his hand and took the nipple in his mouth, circling the pebbled hardness with his tongue. He did the same with the other, exploring and tasting, while the need engorged him until his jeans became tight, painful bands.

He reached down to unzip them. Dani fit her hand over his, their fingers tangling until the zipper gave way and his erection burst free. She fit her hand around it, tugging it from his shorts, and he had to hold his breath to keep from erupting long before he was ready.

He slid a hand between her legs, caressing her through the silk with his fingertips while he slipped the other hand inside the elastic at her waist. "These have to go."

"Yes. Yes." She rose to her elbows and kissed him again as he slid the bottoms down her legs and over her feet. Once they were added to the pile, she opened her legs and he got his first look at the treasure—the hot, wet, pulsing center of her passion. Passion that was all for him.

He buried his face in the sweetness, tasting and teasing with his tongue until she moaned and called his name. He was hit with a need so powerful it tore his breath away.

"Take off your jeans, Marcus. I want all of your gorgeous, muscular masculinity lying naked beside me."

She didn't have to ask twice. He slid off the bed, wiggled out of them and crawled back into bed beside her.

Most men had vivid memories of the first time they'd had sex. Marcus didn't. He re-membered where—under the bleachers of the high school gym his freshman year. But he didn't remember the rush of release or the name of the girl he'd been with. He hated to admit it, but the girl hadn't mattered. It was all about the hormones.

Tonight was different in every way. Tonight was about Dani and an attraction so intense it etched its way into the very core of his being.

No matter what happened between them after this, he'd remember and hold on to every detail for the rest of his life.

DANI WATCHED AS MARCUS shed his jeans and boxers. His body was sheer magnificence. But he was a lot more than muscle, sinew and masculinity. He was her cowboy warrior. Gentle but tough with the soul of a protector and the fiery touch of a lover.

He crawled back into bed and straddled her. His hands found her breasts and cradled them as his thumbs massaged the nipples' pebbly ridges. They were tender from the sensations he'd created in them, yet she arched toward him, craving more.

She reached for his erection and wrapped both hands around the full length of him. She rolled her fingers over his tip and he writhed in her hand.

"Guide me inside you, Dani," he whispered. "I can't hold off any longer."

She understood completely. She'd never been more ready to feel a man inside her. She spread her legs and tugged him toward her waiting depths. He thrust once and buried himself deep. She moaned at the impact and the thrill of the emotions coursing through her. He thrust again, and again, building a rhythm that was carrying her higher and higher.

His breathing became heavy. Her heart pounded. And then he rocked her over the top in an explosion of passion that left her trembling and gasping for breath.

They lay together for long minutes, basking in the afterglow of spent passion.

Marcus finally stirred. “Was it enough?”

“It was everything, Marcus. Everything and more.”

He was her cowboy hero in every sense of the word. She still didn’t understand why she’d fallen so hard or so fast, fallen even before she’d seen how marvelous he really was. And she couldn’t let it matter that this could never last.

She had this moment in time, and the memories would warm her heart for a lifetime.

DANI WOKE TO THE ODORS of sizzling bacon and brewing coffee and the delightful sounds of birds singing outside the open window. Shafts of sunlight danced across the bed. She stretched and turned to look at the clock, and the memories dancing through her mind made her warm and tingly.

Ten minutes after eight. She never slept this late.

But then she never had nights like this at home. She and Marcus made love three times. The second after only the briefest recovery time from the first. The third was when she woke in the wee hours of the morning to the heated ecstasy of Marcus's hands exploring her naked body.

Every intimacy they'd shared had been deliciously exciting and intensely fulfilling. If her pajamas were not still on the floor and her body not reveling in the sweet, tender aches of lovemaking, she might think it had all been a dream.

She reached for Marcus's pillow and hugged it to her before finally pushing the covers away and throwing her legs over the side of the bed. She padded to the bathroom in her bare feet and stared at her reflection in the mirror.

Amazingly the only difference in how she looked was the disheveled state of her hair and the slightly kiss-swollen lips. You'd think making love the way they had last night would have made more noticeable changes. You'd think that kind of passion would glow and shimmer on her skin.

She splashed her face with cold water, and then she thought of Ella Somerville and the fear that had shadowed her eyes in the ICU. Dani's spirit fell into an immediate and drastic downward spiral. The woman was scared to death, so why had she so vehemently turned down Dani's offer of paid protection?

Ella wanted Dani out of her life. The visions wanted her in it.

She didn't understand the full meaning of the psychic communications, but she knew that she and Ella were bound in some inexplicable way. For the first time she admitted the truth to herself. She had to find Ella before the killer did. It might be the only way to save herself.

She slipped on her pajamas, grabbed her robe and slippers and joined Marcus in the kitchen. He was fully dressed in jeans and a black T-shirt that accentuated his six-pack abs. The sight of him rocked her equilibrium.

"Sorry I slept so late."

"I figured I'd worn you out."

Marcus speared the last piece of bacon from the skillet and leaned down to give her a kiss. Quick, but still she felt its heat from her lips to her toes.

"I think it was you who went straight from orgasm to snoring that last time," she said.

"I don't snore."

"Uh-huh. Keep telling yourself that."

Actually, he didn't. She wasn't sure he ever slept that sound. She hated to move in the night, knowing he'd wake.

She opened the refrigerator door and rummaged until she found a jar of homemade blackberry jam Cutter's aunt had made. "What else do we need?"

"Butter for the biscuits."

"You made biscuits?"

"Sort of. I took them out of the freezer and put them in the oven. They're almost ready. How do you like your eggs?"

"I don't. But I love biscuit and bacon sandwiches with oodles of jam." She poured herself some coffee and added a warmer portion to Marcus's mug. "I want to make a quick call to the hospital before we eat and find out if Ella checked herself in again."

"I can save you the trouble. I just talked to them. The answer is no." Marcus broke a couple of eggs into a hot skillet. "But there is good news of sorts. The police located the car that was stolen from the hospital yesterday."

"When? Where?"

"A patrolman noticed it parked on a side street in Old Town Spring during the middle of the night. He hadn't seen a car parked there after the stores closed before, so he ran the license plates and found out it was stolen."

"They found the car, but not Ella?"

"They're not even sure that she's the car thief."

"What about fingerprints? Can't they just check the steering wheel and tell if she drove it?"

"They dusted for prints, but unless hers are on file, they won't be able to match them even if she did steal the car." Marcus served up his eggs and carried them to the table while Dani retrieved the golden-topped biscuits from the oven.

"A pair of jeans and a blue sweater were missing from the car. The rest of the purchases were lying on the backseat."

"Which is proof in my mind that Ella stole the car. She'd need that change of clothes. What about the robe Ella was wearing when she left the hospital?"

"No sign of it," Marcus said.

"Where or what is Old Town Spring?"

"Spring's a small town just south of The Woodlands, about an hour's drive from here.

Old Town is the historic area that has been revived with boutiques, specialty shops and quaint dining spots—or so I've heard."

"What about hotels or motels?"

"I checked. There are several within a three-mile radius of where they found the car. No registrations in her name, but I didn't expect there would be."

Dani buttered a biscuit and slathered it with jam before tucking two slices of crispy bacon inside it. The night's excitement had left her ravenous in spite of her anxiety for Ella.

"Investigating and cooking. You've been busy this morning," she said. "How long have you been up?"

"A couple of hours. I don't need much sleep."

Apparently. She took a bite of the biscuit and then licked her lips to get every crumb while the news about Ella played in her mind. "We need to go to Spring."

"Now how did I know you'd say that?"

"Must be psychic."

"Can we finish breakfast first?"

"Take your time, as long as you're ready in about ten minutes."

She took another bite of her biscuit then wrapped the rest in her napkin and carried it and her coffee with her as she rushed back to the bedroom to get dressed. If they could track Ella to Spring, then Kevin Flanders probably could, too. She had to find a way to convince the deputies he should be arrested. Then Ella would feel safe enough to return to the hospital and all their problems would be solved.

"YOU SAY SHE LOOKS like you. No. Haven't seen her."

"Hon, I've been so busy today I wouldn't have noticed the president coming in unless he skipped out on his check."

"A woman with long auburn hair bought a

chocolate cake from me this morning, but she was at least fifty and wearing a warm-up suit."

"I haven't seen anyone who fits that description, but I've been refilling stock all morning. Talk to one of the clerks."

"I wish I could help you, but I haven't seen her. Did you try the tearoom?"

"Well, my goodness, why didn't you say she was injured in the first place? There was a woman who paid her check and left here not five minutes ago who'd lost her arm in a car wreck. But, no. She had blond hair, so that couldn't be her."

Same results, different speakers and stories. After almost five hours of checking every hotel or motel in the area, then hitting every eating establishment, bakery, coffee shop or grocery store, Dani was beginning to think Ella had either never been in the area or had only made a pit stop before stealing another car and moving on.

Unless they were mistaken about the stolen

car angle and she had been abducted from the hospital. But not by Kevin, unless he'd already killed her and dumped the body before they'd talked to him last night.

Marcus tugged her to a stop before she could step in the path of an SUV pulling away from a gas pump.

"Thanks," she murmured.

"Are you okay or was that a clairvoyant moment?"

"Unfortunately, that was a macabre moment. There have been no clairvoyant moments this morning, not even a vibe that we're getting close to finding Ella. I'm beginning to doubt she's in the area."

"You could be right," Marcus agreed, "but if she's as medically fragile as the doctor indicated, I wouldn't think she'd feel like doing a lot of traveling."

"Or walking," Dani said. "But no clerks admitted to checking anyone meeting her description into a hotel in this area. Perhaps we should check with every taxi driver to see if they picked her up and dropped her off at a hotel in The Woodlands or maybe Conroe."

"Or maybe Houston."

Dani groaned. "And then it might take weeks to find her. I don't even want to think about that."

"We have to consider that possibility," Marcus said, "along with her options for catching a flight or hopping on a bus. I think we should have lunch and regroup."

"Didn't we just have breakfast?"

"About six hours ago."

"Okay, but since we're here, we may as well talk to the clerk in this convenience store. It's near enough to where we found the car that Ella could have walked here to pick up a few groceries. She has to eat."

Dani waited until the customers in line had been taken care of before moving to the counter.

"Can I help you?"

"I hope so. I'm looking for my sister. She has a mental disability and wanders off sometimes and can't find her way home again." It was the best script she'd come up with over the course of the morning.

"Lady, I just take the money. I don't keep up with the customers or test their IQs."

"I just need to know if you've seen her."

He shrugged. "What does she look like?"

"A lot like me except that her hair is longer, a rich auburn color and curly."

The guy studied her, looking more perplexed by the second. He bent over and retrieved something from beneath the counter. "Is this your sister?" he asked, slapping a snapshot down in front of her.

The girl in the photo looked exactly like Dani, same hair, but longer. Same color. No curls. "Where did you get that?"

"A man came in about a week ago looking

for this woman. He said he'd heard she was in this part of Texas, and he seemed real desperate to find her. If you weren't standing here telling me different, I'd swear you're the lady in this photo. If not, you gotta be her twin."

Marcus picked up the photo and held it away from the glare. "Did the man say why he was looking for her?"

"Nope."

"Can you describe him?"

"Hardly. I see hundreds of people a day. Tall, short, every ethnic group you can name."

"Try to remember," Dani pleaded.

"If I told you anything, I'd be making it up."

"Did he say what the woman's name was?" Marcus asked.

"Helena something or other, but he said she probably wasn't going by that. I figure she's an old girlfriend he's trying to hook up with again. But I don't guess so if you say she's your sister and that's she's mentally disabled."

"You must have caught him on the security camera when he came in and gave you the picture." Marcus took out his wallet. "What would it take to get a look at that?"

The clerk stuffed his hands in his pockets. "Sorry. I just work here. Management collects the film and sends it all to the home office. But if you want to give me your name and phone number, I'll let you know if I see this woman."

Dani pulled her business card from her handbag. "Please give me a call if she shows."

"Yeah, sure. I need to wait on some customers now."

A woman pushed by them and set a large bottled soda and a package of chips on the counter, and the clerk went back to business as usual.

Dani was more confused and uneasy than ever when they left the store. "That photo looked exactly me, but it isn't. I've never had a blouse like that, and I haven't worn my hair that long in years."

"The resemblance was striking," Marcus agreed.

"It's freakish. And the man was looking for Helena," she said, "just like in my nightmarish vision."

"The vision where the son of a bitch came after *you,*" Marcus muttered through clenched teeth.

"I don't get it. The photo has to be of Ella, when she weighed a little more, but it couldn't be Kevin that was in here a week ago. He was living with Ella then."

"I'm almost sure it wasn't Kevin," Marcus said. "But I'd love to get my hands on the man and find out why he's looking for her."

"The way you got your hands on Kevin Flanders and Billy Germaine?"

"No. This time I'd take off the velvet gloves."

The new information was disturbing, but it didn't change Dani's mind about Kevin

Flanders. She'd never sensed that fierce brand of evil before. If anyone involved with Ella had the heart of a killer, it had to be him.

PETE MALLORY WATCHED the man and woman walk to the corner and cross the street going west. He didn't buy that bull about her sister being missing. He didn't know what her game was, but she was the same woman in the snapshot.

Pete took care of the next customer and then reached under the counter for the second photo, the one he hadn't shown them. The one with the man's contact number on it.

Ethan Marks had promised a cool five hundred dollars for information leading to his finding the woman in the snapshot. Pete punched the number into his phone. Five hundred dollars would make a payment on his car and leave money left over for a couple cases of beer.

IT WAS PAST THE NOON HOUR and the neighborhood Mexican restaurant was practically empty. Marcus asked for the back booth, one that let him see what was going on inside and outside the restaurant. They both ordered from the lunch menu and then Dani headed to the restroom.

Marcus took out his cell phone and punched in the number for his tech contact. No answer, but he left a message for Eduardo. He needed a list of any abandoned houses or businesses in the Old Town area—any place where Ella might be hiding out.

The next call was to the deputy in charge of the stabbing investigation. As soon as Marcus got past the formalities with Ted, he filled him in on their morning—except for the conversation with that last convenience store clerk. He wasn't quite ready to throw that development into the common-knowledge pool.

"I don't suppose the Spring Police Department has come up with any leads."

"Not yet," Ted said. "I'm sure they're as short-handed as all the other police departments in the country, so I don't expect any superfast results."

Neither did Marcus. "I'd like you to run a missing persons check to see if Ella Somerville fits any of the descriptions in the system."

"I can put a deputy on that this afternoon, but I think it's a waste of time. I'm ninety-nine percent sure Kevin Flanders is our man. All I need is enough evidence to make the arrest."

So Dani wasn't the only one convinced of Kevin's guilt.

"Remember, this is confidential information," Ted continued. "The only reason I can tell you is that the sheriff gave you and Cutter security clearance."

"I realize and appreciate that. What happened with Kevin's alibi?"

"It has serious holes in it. Billy Germaine claims he was playing poker with him and some of his buddies."

"He wasn't?"

"He was there at some point, but none of the other three guys is willing to swear that he was there the exact time of the stabbing."

"What about motive?"

"That's the holdup. We don't have one yet. If we did, Kevin Flanders would be looking out from between narrow bars. But he's a hothead who can fly into a rage over nothing. Everybody says that. He was sporting a few unexplained bruises and two black eyes when I questioned him today."

"I'm sorry to hear that."

"Did you give them to him?"

"Me? I'm just an easygoing P.I. I can't believe you'd even ask."

"Don't mess with me, Marcus. I know what you're capable of. But watch your step. Kevin will not be a pushover for your special ops antics."

"I'll bear that in mind."

"Make sure Ms. Baxter does the same. She has no business getting involved with Ella Somerville and no idea how dangerous messing around with a man like Kevin can get."

Unfortunately, that's where Ted was wrong. Dani knew better than any of them what was at stake. She'd seen it firsthand, over and over again.

The waitress brought their drinks. Black coffee for him. Diet soda for Dani. Five minutes later, Marcus's anxiety started to climb. Dani should have been back from the restroom by now.

He crossed the restaurant and pushed the door to the ladies' restroom open a crack. "Dani."

No answer.

He burst through the door. She was leaning against the sink staring into space. He called her name again, but she gave no indication that she heard him.

She'd fallen into yet another terrifying trance.

Chapter Twelve

The room was little bigger than a closet, shadowed and dank and smelling of mildew and rot. She huddled in the corner, draped in a maroon bathrobe but still shivering. Pieces of broken pottery were scattered about the floor, a frog's head staring up at her.

She pulled up her feet to clear a path for a huge rat that scurried past her. Wadded wrappers and scraps of food from the sandwich she'd had for dinner last night lay a few feet away. Black cockroaches were feeding on the fetid meat.

The rodents and insects were the least of her worries. Pain consumed her body and her head ached to the point she could barely think. Blood oozed from the wound. She raised the water bottle to her feverish lips, and the last few drops trickled down her parched throat.

If she didn't get help, she was going to die. If she went back to the hospital, he'd find her and kill her. There was no way out. There really never had been.

THE ROW OF STALLS that stretched in front of Dani slowly floated into focus. It took a few seconds more before she realized Marcus was standing beside her, steadying her with a strong arm around her shoulder.

A woman walked into the bathroom, saw Marcus and jumped in surprise before glaring at both of them accusingly.

"There was an emergency," Marcus explained. "We'll be out of your way in just a minute."

"I'm okay," Dani murmured. "We can go now."

"Are you sure?"

She nodded, then took a deep, shaky breath.

He kept his arm around her as they walked back to the table, probably afraid she was still woozy. She was but not so disoriented that she didn't know what had to be done.

She stared at the food waiting for them on the table and her head began to swim. "I need fresh air. You eat and I'll wait on you outside."

"Forget eating," Marcus said. "Just sit tight a minute."

He motioned to the waitress and asked for the check, assuring her that their abrupt leaving had nothing to do with the food or service.

"Another vision?" he asked once they were both seated in the truck.

"Yes, but different from the others."

"No green dress?"

"No, and this time it was definitely about Ella."

"Are you ready to talk about it?"

"The sooner the better. There's no time to waste."

IT WAS THREE HOURS and a dozen tours of ratty, abandoned buildings and warehouses later when Marcus talked Dani into stopping again to eat. This time he chose a steak house. He was running on empty. She was running on anxiety and desperation.

Today alone was enough to make him hate these malicious visions that provided enough facts to drive Dani to action and not enough specifics to make her efforts productive. This psychic phenomena business needed some serious overhauling.

Having your life interrupted even once a year or so by this kind of danger magnet would drive a lot of people over the edge. Dani was an extraordinary woman.

No matter that the last vision was about Ella, Marcus was convinced that Dani was still in jeopardy and would continue to be as long as she was entangled with Ella and her would-be killer. There was about as much chance of her backing out before this was over as there was of him leaving her on her own. Basically, zero.

Another concern had plagued him since he'd seen that snapshot in the convenience store. If that snapshot was of Ella, then at the time it was taken, she and Dani were almost identical. That bond Dani kept talking about might not be purely psychic after all.

When the waiter came, Dani ordered the small filet mignon with a garden salad. Marcus went for the biggest sirloin on the menu with a fully loaded baked potato, a salad and some fried calamari as a starter.

"You have a healthy appetite," she said.

"Always have, even in combat. It keeps your strength up. You need to eat, too, or at least try."

"It's hard to look at food, much less eat it, with all these images roaming my mind. It makes me sick that I don't know what to do, but everything is so different this time around. I know I'm supposed to help Ella, but I'm blocked at every turn."

"Have the visions ever been this vague and confusing before?"

"No. Ordinarily, the visions deal with people I know, not strangers. And while I get involved in other people's lives to a point, it's never to this extent. I've never felt the intensity of fear as I did with Ella or seen the blackness of evil as I did with Kevin."

The waiter reappeared with their drinks, a large basket of bread and a promise that the calamari would be right out.

Dani sipped her diet soda. "I'm totally in Ella's life now at my own expense, and our only bond is based on the fact that she could pass as my double and a chance meeting at the Renaissance festival."

"Not fully by chance," Marcus said. "You had the first vision before you'd even heard of the festival."

"I've thought of that, too. But still, Ella was a total stranger before I started having the visions."

"What happens if you ignore the visions?"

Her eyes became shadowed, tumultuous depths. He reached across the table and took her hands. They were as cold as ice and trembling.

"I'll go through life with Ella's blood on my hands."

Damn! How did he keep leading her to these dark, frightening pits when he was only trying to understand?

The calamari arrived. The waiter served it with a flourish and an attempt to make conversation about a major pileup and resulting oil spill that occurred on I-45 that afternoon. Marcus couldn't decide if the timing was rotten or a godsend.

By the time the waiter walked away, Dani

had regained her composure. She forked some of the calamari onto the small plate in front of her. “Sorry for sounding so morbid,” she said. “I’m just worried about Ella.”

Once their entrées arrived, they stopped talking completely while Marcus dove into a steak that was cooked to perfection. Brown on the outside, pink in the center and so tender he barely needed his knife. Ella ate a few bites, but he got the feeling she was forcing it down.

As soon as the hunger pangs in his stomach were appeased, Marcus’s mind went back to their conversation with the clerk in the convenience store. The snapshot he’d shown them was most likely Ella, but it looked exactly like Dani.

What was the chance that two unrelated people could look that much alike? The thought had been haunting him for the past few hours, even as he and Dani had stalked abandoned buildings that had made it mandatory he keep up his guard every second.

If the dagger-wielding attacker was looking for Ella, then it was more than possible he was following the same leads they were. Police reports on stolen vehicles were easy enough to track now that everything went into a computer base.

More worrisome to him was the fact that someone had been here one week earlier looking for the woman in that snapshot.

Who? And why?

A niggling possibility kept skulking into his thought processes and muddying the works. Could the snapshot in the clerk's possession have been a photo of Dani that she didn't realize had been taken? Had Dani's original mistaken identity been accurate? Had the man who'd attacked Ella Somerville meant to kill Dani? If so, he would have likely figured out by now that he'd made a mistake.

He'd come after Dani in the same ruthless way he'd attacked Ella.

The enemy diversion you have been ignoring will be the main attack. Advice straight from the unofficial serviceman's version of Murphy's Law.

"I know we've been at this for hours," Dani said, interrupting his thoughts. "But I'm not going to give up."

So they'd hit the streets and back alleys again, searching for Ella while he kept a close lookout for an assassin who just might be searching for Dani.

MIDNIGHT CAME AND WENT with no results. They'd widened their perimeter several times, searched every structure they found that might vaguely square with Dani's vision and the new possibilities Eduardo had called in to him just an hour ago. Hopefully Eduardo was asleep by now.

"We'll have to widen the perimeter again or go back and see if we missed a possibility," Marcus said.

"I can't believe Ella walked this far away from where we found the car in her condition. My feet are killing me and I'm healthy."

Marcus tended to agree with Dani, though the amount of time they'd spent on their feet seemed like a Sunday stroll compared to what he'd endured in BUDS training. It was watching the stress and frustration eat away at Dani that was getting to him.

"Too bad that last vision didn't give you a couple of street signs to go on."

"Since it didn't, what do you suggest we do now?"

"The Double M and a bed sound good," Marcus said.

"Later."

"Then I say we drive back to where the stolen car was found and give that area a closer look."

"I'll buy that," Dani said, "plus I'll get to rest my feet while you drive."

He bent over. “Get on my back. I’ll piggy-back you to the truck.”

“Are you kidding? I weigh a hundred and twenty pounds.”

“The weight of a light backpack. I’ve carried worse up steep mountains.” While avoiding enemy fire. At least they hadn’t done that—yet. “Jump aboard, baby. Your chariot awaits.”

“You are being such a good sport about this, but you don’t have to stay with me, Marcus. I’d understand if you left me here and drove back to the Double M. One of us might as well get some sleep.”

That was the one option that had never crossed his mind.

THE ALLEY WHERE THE stolen car had been abandoned looked far creepier in the spooky quiet black of the wee hours of the morning than it had in the daylight. Closed shops, creaking noises that sounded like old men’s bones, a loose shutter banging when it caught a poof of wind.

Dani leaned against the back of a building and stared at the surroundings, trying to put herself in Ella's shoes. Sick. Afraid. Tired.

A cat jumped on a trash can nearby, letting out a moaning cry as the lid rattled and tipped backward. A dog howled in the distance, then another. Dani watched as the cat jumped off the trash can and slinked along the side of the next building before jumping on a low window ledge.

What looked to have been a back stoop had been closed in. A room the size of a closet. Dani's pulse raced, though she knew none of the shops in that block were deserted. They'd checked them too carefully earlier today.

A faded sign hung above the back door. The only letters still legible spelled out CERAM. The last letters were missing.

"Ceramics," Dani said out loud. "An abandoned ceramic shop would explain the pieces of broken pottery on the floor around Ella in my vision."

"Only that shop isn't abandoned."

"The back room could be." She walked over and peered in the window, but every inch of it had been covered in duct tape.

Dani broke into a cold sweat, and she felt as if someone were tightening a vise around her temples. "Ella's in this building, Marcus. I'm not having a vision, but I sense her presence. I know she's in there."

"Let's walk around front," Marcus said, "and just see if it's still a ceramic shop. I don't remember one in this spot, but we've covered a lot of ground today."

They did as he suggested. The building was now an art shop, the windows filled with framed paintings. A sign in the front window proclaimed they'd all been done by local artists. A sign on the front door said closed on

Tuesday. It wasn't abandoned, but it had been closed all day today.

"Art shop or not, I know she's in that back room," Dani insisted. "We have to call the police."

"The authorities are not going to break into a privately owned shop on nothing more than what you claim to sense, Dani. There will be lots of questions, and if they buy into your theory at all, they'll call the shop owners and have them come down and unlock the building."

"That could take hours. We can't wait that long."

"I'm sure I can jimmy the back door open," Marcus said, "but first I'll have to disconnect the alarm system. I'm sure they have one."

"You know how to do that?"

"I'm a man of many talents." They returned to the alley, and he went to work, making her stay out of the open, where he could keep his eye on her.

The wind picked up. The cat yelped and the back door of the stoop blew open and slammed shut.

"It's not even locked," Dani said, rushing toward it.

Marcus grabbed her and held her back. "Me first."

She stayed behind him as he stepped inside. The floor creaked beneath his feet as he aimed the bright beam of his card-size flashlight into the dingy room.

All she saw at first was a row of empty shelves that blocked her view of the left back quadrant of the room. A large, rusty kiln took up most of the front quadrant. She didn't recognize the kiln or the shelves from the vision, but she still had this overwhelming sense of Ella's presence.

"Ella." Dani's voice echoed around them, but there was no answer to her call.

The beam of light panned over the leftover

food. At least a dozen roaches scattered and disappeared beneath the door that appeared to lead to the main shop. A maroon, blood-soaked robe lay in a heap beneath the taped window. The head of a ceramic frog peeked from beneath its edge.

"This is it," she whispered. "This is the room from my vision."

Marcus rounded the empty shelves and directed the light into the hidden corner. A few pieces of broken pottery edged the baseboard. There was nothing else.

They'd found the right room, but Ella wasn't here now. Dani shrank against the wall, bitter disappointment and fatigue settling deep inside her.

"It galls me to think we walked right by this spot earlier today," Marcus said. "I don't know how we missed it. She must have crept in here after closing last evening, spent the night, then stayed through the day."

"I was supposed to find her. It took me too long."

Marcus pulled her limp body into his arms. "Don't even think of blaming yourself for this. You had no part in getting Ella into this mess, but you've given up three days of your life so far to get her out of it."

Marcus tried the door that led to the shop. It was locked tight. "The alarm probably only goes off if that door is opened."

Dani walked over and stooped beside the robe. "Sometime in the few hours since the vision, Ella must have started bleeding more and realized she had to get to a hospital. I know there wasn't this much blood on the robe when I saw it in the vision."

Dani jumped back as a spider crawled from the folds of the fleece. "She had to get from the car to here and had to buy food. I just can't imagine that she walked the streets in the daylight in this robe and no one noticed her."

"I don't think she did." Marcus held up a plastic bag he'd retrieved from behind the shelves. "Macy's. She must have stuffed the robe in the same bag where she found the jeans and sweater. She probably thought leaving the robe in the stolen car would be a dead giveaway."

"Let's check the local hospitals."

"On our way back to the Double M," Marcus said. "It's three in the morning. You can't keep going without rest. You'll collapse. If the unearthly powers that be wanted you to find Ella they should have led you here sooner."

"You said you never give up."

"I don't. Tomorrow's another day, and your collapsing from exhaustion won't help anyone."

She knew he was right, and Ella had her business card. All she had to do was call.

Reaching that conclusion affected Dani like a drug. Her eyes became instantly heavy, and her muscles felt as if they were dissolving.

Even the anticipation of crawling into bed next to Marcus didn't send any titillating signals to her brain.

But still she loved the thought of falling asleep in his strong, protective arms.

MARCUS CAUGHT THREE HOURS of restless sleep before waking to Dani's rhythmic breathing, matched by his own gentle stirrings of desire. Her head was on his shoulder, her silky hair tickling his chin. One bare shapely leg was thrown over his, her knee in a very arousing spot.

She squirmed in her sleep and the knee inched higher. He glanced down and caught a glimpse of her right breast, the nipple bright pink against his tanned, hairy chest. He swallowed a groan at the intensity of his hunger for her.

His cell phone vibrated along the surface of his bedside table and snapped him to attention. He swung his free arm and grabbed the phone to silence the clamor. Extricating his other arm and his leg without waking Dani took a bit more skill.

She squirmed again and rearranged her gorgeous body. Regretfully, he covered her with the sheet and padded from the room to take the call.

"Good morning, Cutter. Don't you folks down at the main house ever sleep?"

"We're on ranching hours. And we weren't up all night."

"We were."

"I know. I heard you drive by near sunup. How did the hunt for Ella Somerville go?"

"It didn't." Marcus filled him in on the details, leaving nothing out, including the fact that as of 4:00 a.m. this morning, Ella had not checked into any hospitals in The Woodlands or Spring areas.

"What do you make of the man showing up at the convenience store looking for the woman in the snapshot?"

The woman in the snapshot. Not Ella. Marcus knew exactly what his partner was thinking because he'd considered the same possibility. "It adds a new twist."

"But you don't think it's a picture of Dani?"

"She insists it isn't," Marcus said.

"Interesting, though, that Ella and Dani look so much alike that even you would have taken the photo to be Dani. You don't usually get that close a resemblance without some shared DNA. If not twins, they could be half sisters. Lots of men spread their seed around, sometimes without knowing themselves that they've sired a child."

"Dani's never mentioned a father or a mother for that matter."

"But the possibility of her and Ella being related has surely crossed your mind, too?"

"Not until I saw the snapshot," Marcus said honestly.

"Birth records are easy to check these days.

If you don't have time to run an Internet search, Eduardo can handle it."

Yeah. Marcus knew that, too. He just hated to throw more curves at Dani right now if they weren't related to the mystery at hand. The problem was they might well be.

"I'll keep Eduardo in mind."

"Regardless of who's in the photo, I'm sure you've considered that the mystery man might have stabbed Ella because he mistook her for Dani," Cutter mused.

"Every second since I saw the photo. It raises the stakes in the game considerably if Dani is the target victim."

"Raises the stakes because she's the one you've been paid to protect?"

"Sure. What else?"

"Get off it, Marcus. You're talking to me, remember. Cutter Martin, the guy who knows you better than you know yourself. You're falling for Dani and you know it. Not that I can lecture you about that with a clear conscience. I did the same with Linney. Just be careful. Keep the odds in your favor. Remember, if you find yourself in a fair fight, you didn't plan your mission properly."

"Yeah, buddy. I'll stay on top of things. Now how about you? How'd things go with Homeland Security?"

"I'm meeting with them again today, but it looks like a done deal. They need our expertise and ability to go undercover into situations they can't. And I heard from Hawk again. Looks like he'll be joining up with us, maybe operating a field office. I'll fill you in on everything when we can sit down together and talk."

"Works for me."

The temptation to crawl back in bed with Dani was almost overpowering. But once he was there, he'd never be satisfied to let her sleep, and she needed her rest. The visions took a physical as well as emotional toll on her, and he doubted they were through with her yet.

Instead he made a pot of coffee, opened his laptop and logged onto the Internet. Birth records were indeed easy to trace. He was deep into the research an hour later when Dani walked into the kitchen wearing nothing but one of his T-shirts.

His libido kicked in. The facts he'd discovered tamped them back down. He walked over, kissed her good morning and poured her a cup of coffee.

"Any news?" she asked.

"Yeah, but you might want to sit down before I lay it on you."

Chapter Thirteen

Dani stared at the computer printout Marcus had dropped on the table near her coffee cup. She took a long sip of the brew before tackling this new bit of news. Whatever it was, she had a feeling it wasn't good.

A birth certificate.

Mother's Name: Janice Marie Alano

Father's Name: None provided

Her mother. Her lack of a father. She stopped reading. She'd seen this all before, had a copy in her personal records at home.

"Why would you look up my birth certificate?"

Marcus pulled a chair next to hers and straddled it. "Keep reading."

He'd highlighted another entry. She scanned it quickly.

Again it was her mother's name. No father. Same date from thirty-three years ago. Live birth of a female. Only this time there was the notation that the baby was unnamed. "I don't get it."

"Check the time of birth."

She did. Four minutes later for the unnamed infant than was on her certificate. Same Minden, Louisiana, hospital. Same attending physician.

"There must be a mistake. It looks as if my mother gave birth to two babies that night."

Marcus waited without saying a word while the truth pushed its way past the emotional hurdles she'd erected. Two births. Twins. One was Dani, the other unnamed. Baby no-name.

She swallowed hard. She'd taken her grandmother's statement for the ramblings of senility. But when Dani had started talking about someone who looked just like her, Grams had merely let her mind return to the same bygone years where she spent so much time these days.

"If this is accurate, then the second baby must have died right away," Dani said, trying to get a handle on this. "She could have been born sickly. That's likely why they didn't name her."

"But no one ever mentioned that to you?"

"No. Not once." An odd fact to keep secret. She took another sip of the coffee and toyed with the mug handle while her mind grappled with the new information. Finally, it dawned on her where Marcus was going with this.

"You think Ella could be my twin sister, don't you? That's why you looked up all of this."

"I think it's a possibility," Marcus said. "Ella could have been given up for adoption right after she was born. If your parents had chosen to keep it secret, you'd have had no way of knowing you were a twin."

She shook her head. "Why give up one baby and keep the other? If you don't want children, give them both up."

"Maybe they were having a hard time financially and didn't think they could afford to raise two children."

"There wasn't a *they.* My father's name isn't listed because he was never in the picture. When I asked about him as a child, I was told he was dead. Later, Grams told me my mother had never been sure who he was. Apparently she was big into one-night stands."

"I'm sorry."

"Don't be, at least not for that. I've long since quit caring."

"If your mother was alone, she may not have felt capable of caring for two babies."

"She wasn't alone. We lived with Grams until..."

No, she wasn't going there with Marcus. She was vulnerable enough as it was. And now she had all of this to deal with. Why would Marcus even bother to research this unless he thought their being twins had something to do with the attack on Ella?

"Ella didn't draw me into this, Marcus. She never wanted my help. I came charging into this on my own."

"You didn't exactly charge in on your own," he reminded her. "You were pulled in by the visions."

Marcus's grasp on this was better than her own right now. The visions had linked them together. The psychic connection with Ella made no sense before. But if they were related, if Ella was her twin…

Oh, God. Ella could actually be her twin sister. She should be ecstatic—or angry at the deception, or at least disconcerted. The truth was she felt numb, as if she were slipping into a state of shock.

Marcus slid a hand over hers. "Maybe I shouldn't have mentioned this at all."

"Why did you? You must have good reason for giving up much-needed sleep to dredge up my past this way." She pulled away from him as a wave of frustration took hold. "You still don't fully trust me, do you?"

"Trust has nothing to do with this. I just don't like the odds of trying to protect you when I don't have a handle on all the facts."

"The facts are that Kevin Flanders wants Ella Somerville dead. Whether I'm her long-lost twin sister or the Queen of England, it won't change that."

He stood and threw his arms in the air as if he were ready to throw in the towel and wash his hands of her altogether. She'd known that was inevitable. She just hadn't expected it quite this soon. She stood to go back to the bedroom to dress.

He grabbed her arm and tugged her to a stop. "Your vision two nights ago showed *you* in danger, Dani. *You* were the one in that green dress. *You* were the one being attacked. And now I find that some guy has been traveling around this part of Texas searching for a woman who looks just like you."

"It's not me in the photo. I told you that."

"And just how is he supposed to know the difference when I couldn't even tell it wasn't you? We don't know why he's so eager to find Ella or who else might be searching for her. She could have witnessed a crime or stolen drug money from a dealer or blackmailed some politician. The man who's looking for her could be a paid assassin."

"So how nice of you to find out that I'm her twin."

His voice lowered, became gruff and edgy. “I need facts to keep you safe, Dani. I need to know what the hell I’m up against and if that means digging up your past, so be it. I’ll dig up the remains of Abraham Lincoln if that’s what it takes.”

Emotion overtook her. She was fighting for Ella’s life. Marcus was, too, but his real fears were for her. Tears burned the back of her eyes, and she stood and stepped into his arms.

“I’m sorry, Marcus.”

He rocked her to him. “I should have found a better way to tell you this or not told you at all until things were back to normal.”

“No, I needed to know. It explains so much.”

She started to pull away. “I should get dressed.”

His hold on her tightened. “Not yet. Let’s go back to bed, Dani. Not to make love, not unless you want to. I need to lie beside you and hold you in my arms for a few precious minutes. Then we’ll discuss our next move.”

"If we go back to bed together, you know what our next move will be."

He nuzzled his lips against the curve of her neck. "Would that be so bad?"

"No, it wouldn't be bad at all."

The distinctive sound of an approaching car interrupted the moment. "Even on a ranch you can't get any privacy," Marcus complained as he walked to the window, opened the blinds and looked out. "It's the deputies who questioned you the other night."

"Ted and Greg. I hope they've come to tell us Kevin's been arrested."

"Unless they've discovered some concrete evidence against him, they couldn't keep him over twenty-four hours anyway."

"That's absurd. He's a prime suspect."

"It's called innocent until proven guilty."

"That's a lousy way to run a sheriff's department." Dani refilled her mug with the hot brew.

"I'll be back to hear what they have to say as soon as I throw some clothes on."

"There goes that fantasy."

A fantasy probably was the very best word to describe their relationship since it had the lasting power of a snowball in south Texas.

Her mind went back to the morning's discovery. If by some wild chance Ella was her twin, it would explain why the visions had connected them when Ella was in danger. It would also explain the instant bond she'd felt with her, the overwhelming sense that they'd met before.

It would even clarify the confusing images that had troubled her as a young child, the ones her mother had reprimanded her for and accused her of making up. Thinking she'd fallen from a tree when she hadn't. Begging to go back to a park her mother had insisted didn't exist.

And on and on.

Grams had undoubtedly understood that she was making a psychic connection with the twin sister she'd never known. She'd comforted Dani, but even she never mentioned a baby given up for adoption. Eventually, the connections stopped altogether. Until now.

Dani sighed and tried to understand why her mother gave up one of the two girls born to her that night. What a shock and disappointment it must have been for her when she realized that the child she'd chosen to keep was psychic. No wonder her mother hated her.

Whether Ella was her twin or not, the important thing now was saving her life. DNA testing to determine their relationship could come later—if it came to that.

BY THE TIME THE TWO deputies were seated at the small kitchen table, mugs of coffee in hand, Dani reappeared. Marcus marveled that she'd dressed so quickly in a straight brown skirt and a pale sweater the color of a sun-drenched hay field.

She hadn't bothered with makeup, and he had to wonder why she ever did. She looked just as terrific without it, maybe even better. Good enough to make a man drool. In fact, Greg practically was. He hadn't taken his eyes off Dani since she'd stepped into the room and greeted them with a wary smile.

Time to get down to business.

Marcus held a chair for Dani but kept standing himself. "I'm sure you guys didn't just stop by for free coffee. What's up?"

"More to the point, have you arrested Kevin Flanders?" Dani asked.

Ted sipped his coffee before answering. "No, but we must be doing something right. We had a visit from Kevin's attorney late yesterday afternoon, a poor man's shark right down to the sleazy suit with the shiny finish. He accused us of harassing his client."

Greg grinned and scratched a pimply spot on his ruddy cheek. "We're still considering Kevin a person of interest, and we're heading over to question him again when we leave here."

"He's not a person of interest," Dani protested. "He's the person who stabbed Ella Somerville, and you're letting him walk around a free man so that he can finish what he started."

"Unfortunately, Ella may have done that for him," Ted said. "She was found unconscious and lying in an alley this morning in Old Town Spring. A trash crew discovered her and called 911."

"Where is she now?" Dani demanded, her voice shaky.

Marcus rounded the table and stepped behind her chair, resting his hands on her shoulders. He felt her tremble and hated that there seemed to be no end to this.

"An ambulance took her back to the same hospital she'd walked away from," Ted explained. "She's lost more blood, and the stabbing wound's become infected. The word is it will be touch and go for the next twenty-four hours."

"Is there a guard at her door?"

"She's not going anywhere. She's not even conscious."

"But what's to keep Kevin from going there?"

Greg leaned forward and propped his elbows on the table. "You don't have to worry about Kevin. Anywhere he goes, we're going to know about it. We got a tail on him 24/7. Best thing that can happen would be for him to try something now."

Ted pushed back from the table. "You can just relax here at the ranch for a few days or go on back to Austin when you're ready, Ms. Baxter. We've got everything under control."

"I appreciate your coming by and filling us in on this," Marcus said.

"No problem." Ted stood and clapped Marcus on the back. "I been knowing Cutter Martin all his life. When he says you're one of us, you're one of us. We'll keep you in the loop."

Marcus thanked them again as he walked with them to the door and then hurried back to Dani. He'd just given her a twin sister. Now death might steal her away before she had a chance to find out for certain if that sister was Ella Somerville.

Dani was washing the cups when he returned to the kitchen. "I want to go to the hospital."

"They may not let have Ella have visitors. Even if they do, she's unconscious."

"I know. I just want to be there with her. And I know what the deputies said about tailing Kevin, but that's not good enough. I want a guard at the door to the ICU. I'll pay."

"I'll call and make the arrangements. How about breakfast before we leave for the hospital?"

"Just more black coffee for me. I couldn't eat, but you go ahead. You really don't have to go with me. You must have other business you need to attend to. I'll be fine alone."

She still didn't get it. Nothing he could possibly have to do was more important than being with her until all of the pieces of this complex puzzle fell into place and he was certain she was safe.

Even then it would be pure hell to let her go.

"YOU AND MR. ABBOT may go in now, Ms. Baxter, but you can only stay five minutes. You can talk to Ms. Somerville, but don't say anything that might upset her. She opens her eyes from time to time, but we're not sure how much she's hearing and comprehending."

"I understand."

Her pulse quickened as she stepped through the door and approached the hospital bed. Ella's face had only slightly more color than the pillowcase beneath her head. Her eyes were closed, the flesh around them dark and puffy. She looked as if she'd aged years in the past few days.

In spite of all of that, Dani could still see the resemblance between them. It was evident in the shape of her face, the slight upturn of her nose, the bone structure in her cheeks.

Ella actually could be her twin sister. It boggled her mind. Mostly it touched her heart, now that she'd had time to adjust to the idea of it.

"Hello, Ella."

Her eyes fluttered open. Dani's hands started to shake. She leaned close so that her whispered words were for Ella's ears only. "You're going to be okay. No one's going to hurt you. I won't let them." She reached into her pocket for the business card she'd placed there this morning. Hopefully this time Ella would use it if the need arose.

"I'm putting a card in the drawer beside your bed. Call the phone number on it or have the nurse call if you need anything at all."

Reaching to her left, she opened the drawer an inch and dropped the card for the Double M Investigation and Protection Service inside. She'd have to go back to Austin and check on Celeste tomorrow, but Marcus would be close by. Plus he'd be in contact with the guards he was arranging to watch over Ella.

She bowed her head and prayed silently for Ella to pull through this. It was all she could do for her now.

Ella opened her eyes again. This time her deep, haunting gaze locked with Dani's. The fear in them was as palpable as it had been the last time she'd seen her.

"Kev…" The name was all Ella uttered before she closed her eyes again.

Dani's heart skipped erratically, and a thick haze began to fill the hospital room.

"Forget it, Billy. I've paid you all I'm going to. I got you this job. But that's it. No more cash. No more drugs."

"You don't call the shots. I do."

"Not anymore. I've had enough of your threats and blackmail."

"They're not threats. One call to the Pensacola Police Department is all it will take."

"Yeah, and what will you tell them? That you watched me kill a guy and then helped me get rid of the murder weapon? That you've been blackmailing me ever since?"

"I don't have to tell them anything. There were plenty of other witnesses in the bar that night. All I have to do is make the call and tell them where to find you. Tell them Kevin Flanders is really the guy they only know as Buck."

"You son of a bitch. If I go down, I won't go alone. I promise you that."

"Get the money, Kev. You have two days."

"Don't threaten me, Billy. I'll tell that dragon-loving girlfriend of yours what you're really like."

"She wouldn't believe you. I've already told her you're a killer on the run."

They both jumped as a door squeaked open and the shadow of a woman climbed the wall behind them.

Dani backed away from the bed, her heart slamming against the walls of her chest. She didn't say another word until she and Marcus had left the ICU.

But she knew now that things were going to work out fine. Ella was going to live. Why else would the psychic powers have brought Dani into this? Why else would they have given her the means to put Kevin Flanders in jail?

"I know his motive, Marcus," she whispered. "I know why Kevin tried to kill Ella and why she knows he'll try again."

"You didn't hear it from Ella. All she said was Kevin's name."

"No, I heard it from Kevin himself."

THEY LEFT THE BUILDING and made a fast retreat to the hospital parking lot where they could talk in private. Bright rays of sunshine warmed the car. Marcus lowered the window and moved his seat back so that he could get comfortable and face Dani.

"I'm sure she was trying to tell me what happened," Dani said. "She was so weak she couldn't get it out. The vision did it for her."

About time the visions came through—if they actually had. He half expected more runaround from them, though Dani appeared more confident about the situation than ever.

"Kevin is wanted for murdering a man in a bar in Pensacola, Florida."

Marcus emitted a low whistle. "Now we're cooking. Tell me more."

"Evidently Billy Germaine was with him when it happened, and he's been blackmailing Kevin."

"You discovered all that from the vision?"

"Yes," Dani said, "but I'm not the only one.

Ella must have overheard the same conversation that I did. That's why he has to kill her."

"Exactly what did you hear?"

She gave him a blow by blow of the vision. The pieces of the puzzle began to slide into place. The man flashing the snapshot around and calling the woman in it Helena still bothered him, but even that could probably be explained. The authorities in Florida had likely gotten word that Kevin had been seen with Ella Somerville and were trying to track her down. They may have had her actual name.

"All we have to do is tell the sheriff that Kevin is wanted for murder," Dani said. "We should call him right now." She pulled her cell phone from her handbag.

Marcus reached across the seat and put a hand over hers to stop her. "What are you going to tell him when he asks how you got hold of this information?"

Her expression grew troubled, and she

dropped the phone to her lap. "I can't tell him the truth. Even if I did he wouldn't believe me."

"Maybe he would."

"No." Worry lines burrowed into her brow. "No one can know I'm a psychic. You promised."

"Okay, take it easy. Telling the truth is not the only way to handle this." Probably not even the best way, but he hated that Dani kept so much hurt bottled inside. Now was not the time to get into that with her.

"So how do we handle it?" she asked.

"We do exactly as Billy Germaine planned to do, with an anonymous tip to the Pensacola Police Department telling them that their murder suspect is being investigated in Texas. They'll call our sheriff. He'll fax them a photo of Kevin, and then Kevin will be arrested."

Marcus returned his seat to the driving position, buckled his seat belt and turned the key in the ignition. "All we need is a prepaid phone that can't be traced back to either of us. And then we just sit back and let the fun begin."

She leaned over, threw her arms around his neck and kissed him, the kind of teasing, tantalizing kiss that only whet his appetite for more.

"You're magnificent, Marcus. I'll never be able to thank you enough for all you've done."

"Don't worry. I'll think of a way."

THE SUN WAS LOW IN THE SKY when they drove through the gates of the Double M Ranch. Marcus had been afraid that with Kevin's arrest imminent, Dani might drive back to Austin that afternoon. He knew she hated being away from Celeste.

They'd returned to Ella's hospital room once Marcus had made the phone call on the untraceable phone and stayed there until the nurses assured Dani that Ella was responding to treatment. Both her temperature and her blood pressure were almost back into normal ranges. At that point, it was so late that Dani had decided to spend one more night in Dobbin.

He could tell she was trying not to get too caught up in the idea of Ella being her twin sister, but whether they were or not, they'd already developed an emotional bond through the visions.

Marcus was just thankful that he'd have another night with Dani. He wasn't nearly ready for her to drive off into the sunset. He was starting to get the feeling that he might never be.

A few days ago he'd been sure he'd never again trust a woman with his heart. A few days ago he hadn't met Dani Baxter. The attraction had been instant and so strong it was scary. Now it was a burning need that never let up.

And it wasn't just the sexual part of their relationship that had his heart kicking around inside him like a bull on a short rope. It was all of her.

The way she looked when she woke up in the

morning, all dewy-eyed and fresh. The way she walked with that sexy little sway to her hips. The way she laughed. The way she connected with Celeste. Even the way she traveled back and forth between this world and the psychic realm intrigued him.

But mostly it was the way she handled whatever was thrown her way. She was sweet and vulnerable, yet tough and determined, all arranged into one gorgeous, dynamic package.

She'd slept most of the way home, but she opened her eyes and stretched as they neared his cabin. "We're here already?"

"Already as in an hour after I was finally able to drag you from the hospital."

"Is it too late to saddle up the horses and ride down to the river?"

"We have another hour of daylight, but you must be exhausted. You got very little sleep last night."

"The catnap helped. But we don't have to go

riding if you're not up to it. You got far less sleep last night than I did."

"An unmarried cowboy never turns down a chance to go riding with a beautiful woman." Besides, they had things to talk about, like where they went from here. The river where they'd shared that first mind-blowing kiss might be just the place to do it.

DANI WANDERED TOWARD the bank of the slow-moving river while Marcus tethered their mounts. She'd asked for this ride, but now she wasn't sure that being out here with him was such a good idea. So much had happened to her the past few days that she could barely register a clear thought. Her feelings for Marcus were tangled up in every aspect of the current confusion and emotional roller coaster.

A pair of deer stepped into the clearing just across the narrow river. She stood perfectly still, trying not to startle them. They watched her for a few seconds, then one turned and ran back into the brush and the other followed close behind.

Most men would have run from her that same way given the intensity of her psychic encounters. Marcus was still here, but she knew better than to believe that could last. Yet she ached to spend one more night in his arms, didn't think she could bear it if she couldn't.

Marcus stepped behind her, wrapped his arms around her waist and pulled her back against his muscular chest. He trailed kisses from her earlobe to her shoulder, sending heated tingles skipping along her nerve endings.

"I wish you weren't going back to Austin tomorrow."

"So do I, but my life is there the same way yours is here."

"It doesn't have to be."

Her nerves grew edgy. She was afraid of where this conversation was going. She hadn't expected this from Marcus. He had his life all worked out. He had to know she'd never fit into it.

"I'm not too good with the mushy stuff, but I'm crazy about you, Dani. I'm guessing you've noticed since I can't keep my hands off you."

"You've been great, Marcus, but…"

"Don't start with the buts until you hear me out. I'm not trying to rope and tie you down this soon, but I'd like to keep seeing you. I'll come to Austin when we both have a free weekend. You and Celeste can come to the Double M whenever you want. No pressure. We'll just see what happens."

The ache went clear to her soul, but she knew what would happen. The same thing that always happened. Not in the next few weeks, but eventually. His leaving would be inevitable.

Walking away from Marcus now would break her heart. Losing him later would destroy her.

"A simple okay will do," he said when her silence stretched on for painful seconds.

She had to push the answer from her throat. "I'd love to keep seeing you, Marcus, but I can't."

His arms dropped from around her. "Guess I misread the signals here. Is there someone else?"

She turned to face him. "There's no one else. How can you even ask that after the way we made love the other night?"

"Then you admit we are great together?"

"Great would be the understatement of the century."

"So what's the problem? That I'm a cowboy instead of some rich Austin businessman?"

"No businessman ever turned me on the way you do, Marcus Abbot. And you're not just a cowboy, except in your mind, even though I'd have no complaints if you were. You're still special ops, just without the official credentials. You and Cutter both thrive on action, on living on the edge."

"So it's my job with Cutter that scares you?"

"No. The problems with our starting a relationship have nothing to do with you. It's me. It's the visions. I never know when or how they'll disrupt my life. Do you really think you could live with that year after year after year?"

"You said you don't have them that often."

"I haven't for the past few years, but there's no guarantee it will stay that way. There's no guarantee of anything with me. I don't control the psychic visitations. They control me."

Shudders shook her body. She was losing control now, and there were no visions to blame it on. "My first marriage ended because Todd couldn't take living with a clairvoyant. The divorce ripped mine and Celeste's life apart. I can't do that to her again. I can't do that to me."

"I'm not Todd. I don't give up when the going gets tough. I thought you knew that about me. I guess I was wrong."

"You have no idea what it's really like to live with a psychic."

"Then why don't you tell me?"

She closed her eyes, fighting back the tears that were forming, fighting back a lifetime of painful memories.

Marcus wrapped his hands around her forearms, gripping so hard his fingers dug into her flesh. "You keep all of this stuff bottled up inside you and use it as a shield against taking charge of your own happiness."

"I don't."

"Don't you? Isn't that what this is really about?"

Damn him. She was the psychic, but he saw right through her. "Okay, Marcus. You want the whole sordid story of my life. Here it is. My grandfather left Grams when my mother was a baby. He couldn't take it. My own mother hated her and blamed her for ruining her life. She hated me for being like Grams and threatened to leave me every time I had a vision.

"Finally she did just that. I was nine years old. She just walked off and never came back."

Marcus let go of her arms and propped his hands on the trunk at her shoulders, pinning her between him and the tree. "Look at me, Dani."

She couldn't. "I don't want your pity."

"For God's sake, look at me and tell me what you see."

She met his penetrating gaze. She saw strength, rock hard. Solid. "I see a man who's not afraid of anything, but…"

"Well, good," he interrupted, "because you're talking like I'm some wimpy panty-waist who can't take the heat."

"It's not about you."

"Fine, then you do what you want, make all the excuses you need to, but don't stand there and tell me that you can't take a chance on us because I won't have the guts to see it through."

He kissed her hard, demanding, almost punishing, and still the thrill of him ran through her in breath-stealing waves. She arched toward him and felt the thrusting hardness of his desire pressing into her abdomen.

The passion dissolved as quickly as it began. He broke off the kiss, muttered a curse and strode away without looking back, leaving her to deal with the myriad of emotions erupting inside her.

The phone call came as they climbed into the saddles. The Pensacola Police Department had gotten in touch with the local sheriff's office. One of their homicide detectives was en route, and Kevin Flanders was under arrest.

The danger was over. She should feel relief, but all she felt was a frigid emptiness deep in her soul.

DANI WOKE IN THE WEE HOURS of the morning, immediately aware of the empty spot beside her where Marcus had slept for the past three nights. She missed his warmth, missed the way he spooned his body around hers while she slept, missed the sound of his breathing.

She should have never made love with him when she knew the relationship had nowhere to go. That was her biggest mistake. She rolled over, pounded her pillow and tried to go back to sleep.

It was useless. She couldn't sleep knowing Marcus was just across the hall. She wondered what he'd do if she knocked on his door right now. Would he open his arms or turn his back on her? Not that she could blame him if he turned her away. He had every right to his anger. But it wasn't as if this weren't hell for her, too. You'd think he'd see that.

This was getting her nowhere. She kicked her legs over the side of the bed, pushed her feet into her slippers and padded into the hall. A shaft of light shone from under Marcus's bedroom door. The ache to crawl into his arms one last time was overpowering. She tiptoed to his door and lifted her hand to knock.

And then what? Make more memories to haunt her the rest of her life? Give them both false hope that they could make this work? She might as well raise a dagger and pierce her own chest.

Nursing a heartache the size of Texas, Dani turned and walked away.

Chapter Fourteen

Linney was on her front porch, having a cup of coffee while she perused the morning newspaper. Dani pulled up in the driveway, killed the engine and got out. She'd make this short.

Linney waved a greeting as Dani trudged the walk and climbed the porch steps.

"You're up and out early this morning," Linney said. "Are you driving back to Austin?"

"I am, but first I'm going to stop by Ella's trailer and then make a fast trip to the hospital to see her."

"Why stop by her trailer?"

"A man from hospital admissions called me a few minutes ago and said they need her insurance papers. Evidently she's talked enough to tell them that the file is in her bedroom closet. He said they have to have the information today or they'll have to discharge her."

"That sounds a little over the top, but I know hospitals are feeling the money crunch, too, these days."

"I guess."

"Have you heard how Ella's doing this morning?" Linney asked.

"She's alert and responding. They think she's past the worst of the life-threatening hurdles."

"What a relief."

"Yes, and did you hear that Kevin Flanders has been arrested?"

"I did. Cutter told me that the Pensacola Police Department tracked him down on murder charges at the exact same time as he was about to be arrested for attempted murder here. Talk about your great timing."

Dani looked around nervously when she heard the rattle and clunk of an approaching tractor. Thankfully, it wasn't Marcus, but she should get out of here before he did show up. She didn't think she could face him this morning without completely falling apart.

"I won't keep you," Dani said. "I just wanted to stop by and thank you for all you've done this week and to tell you again what a great time the girls had with you and the horses."

"I loved having them here. And hopefully the next time you're all here, we won't have a dark knight to deal with."

Dani only managed a nod.

Linney stared at her dubiously. "You are coming back, aren't you?"

Dani took a deep breath and exhaled slowly, hating that her eyes were growing moist. “Probably not, but thanks for the invitation. I’ve got to go. Thanks again—for everything.”

She walked away before Linney could say more.

MARCUS HAD SPENT the hours just after sunrise mending a fence up in the northwest pasture. It was the kind of routine ranching duty that usually cleared his mind and calmed his agitation. It didn’t work today.

He started back to the cabin, then changed his mind and decided to stop off at Cutter’s. He was ready for a new assignment, and not one involving Hollywood horrors. He needed something he could sink his teeth and mind into, preferably something risky and dangerous that kept him on the edge every second of the day.

An assignment that would help push Dani out of his mind.

Linney met him at the back door, hands on

hips, fire in her eyes. "What did you do to run her off?"

All of a sudden he was the bad guy. He hadn't a clue what brought this on. "Did you talk to Dani?"

"Only for a few minutes, but it was clear she was upset and not planning to ever set foot on the Double M again. Well, you just let a great woman walk right out of your life."

"You barely know her."

"I'm a good judge of character, Marcus Abbot, and I'm observant. You two had all the bells ringing. Just because you married a cheating tramp the first time doesn't mean all women are like that. Look at me. I was married to a loser before Cutter, but that didn't keep me from knowing we'd be dynamite together."

"Let it go, Linney. And for the record, you're way off base. Where's Cutter?"

"In the shower. I'll tell him you're here."

Marcus's cell phone vibrated as she walked

away. He checked the caller ID. The call was from the hospital where Ella was a patient. Not a good sign. He answered anyway.

"I'm calling for Marcus Abbot."

The voice was female, the words slightly slurred and so low he could barely hear her.

"You got him."

"This is Ella Somerville. I'm looking at your card. It says Investigation and Protection."

"Yes, but Kevin Flanders is on his way to a jail cell this morning, so I doubt you'll be needing my protection."

"This isn't about Kevin."

"Okay. How can I help you?"

"You were here yesterday with a woman who looks a lot like me."

"Dani Baxter. What about her?"

"It's my husband. He's going to kill her."

DANI PARKED HER CAR near the small, weathered trailer where she and Marcus had the run-in with Kevin. She shuddered as she thought of the evil that had surrounded him. A black heart produces a black aura, Grams always said. Malevolence is opaque and blocks out the light.

The trailer looked even more ramshackle in the bright light of day. Mud-streaked and rusty, it had an abandoned, sinister feel to it.

Yet Ella had lived here with a murderous lover. Had she loved him or had something in her past drove her to settle for so little in a mate? There were lots of things Dani didn't know about Ella. If it turned out that she was Dani's twin, she hoped to spend lots of quality time getting acquainted, that is if Ella wanted any part of her.

A twin sister. It was still hard to believe it might be possible. Grams would finally get to meet her no-name granddaughter, though it wouldn't surprise Dani a bit to find out Grams had kept up with Ella telepathically through the years.

Dani had turned her phone off when she'd left the Double M, afraid Marcus would call and she'd have to struggle through a heartbreaking goodbye. She'd been just as afraid he wouldn't call. Either way, she'd have ended up in tears.

She was tempted to check and see if he'd left a message, but this time she let her good sense rule. She dropped the phone into the car's canister where she kept her CDs.

An icy chill swept through her as she climbed the two metal steps. Goosebumps peppered her arms. Her stomach clenched.

It was just the dust of evil left behind by Kevin. There was nothing to fear now that he was in jail. His friend Billy might walk in on her, but she doubted it. He'd make himself scarce with Kevin under arrest, be afraid that Kevin would make good on his promise to take him down with him.

She tried the door. It was unlocked and opened easily. Once inside, she felt an overpowering sensation that someone was inside the trailer with her, watching her every move.

The anxiety swelled until she found it difficult to breathe. She was tempted to turn around and leave. Surely admissions could wait on insurance information. But then you never knew with hospitals.

"Is anyone here?" Her voice echoed down the short, cluttered hallway, but there was no response. Forcing the irrational fears aside, she maneuvered her way toward the bedroom. She'd locate the paperwork and be on her way.

The Pensacola newspapers were gone. So was the feathered, green hat that had hung above them. The door to the bedroom was ajar. She shoved it and it squeaked open. Her gaze fell on the bed and the jade-green velvet dress that had been laid out as if for a ball.

Or for a corpse.

Panic seized her and turned her muscles to liquid. She tried to run but a hand reached out from behind the door and locked around her arm.

"Finally, we meet again, but you don't look pleased, my sweet Helena."

Her heart slammed against her chest. She turned and stared at the man whose grasp was cutting into her flesh like knives. It was the man who'd been watching her that first day at the festival, and the aura swirling around him was thick as smoke and black as night.

She forced the words past the choking knot in her throat. "You have the wrong person. I'm not Helena."

"Oh, come now, my love, don't think you can play me for a fool. You almost got that red-haired strumpet killed by fixing her up to look like you. It might have worked had I not seen you that same night, talking to the police like you were completely innocent. Of course, they believed you. Everyone always believed you. Even me."

She tried to break free, but he yanked her arm behind her back and twisted until she cried out and bent over in pain. She had to find a way to reason with him. "My name is not Helena. I don't know what you're talking about."

"Now, now, sweetheart, did you really think you could just disappear and that I wouldn't come looking for you? I'm your husband. I loved you."

Husband. He and Ella must have been married, might still be. No wonder she could live with Kevin. She was used to worse. "I'm not your wife. My name is Dani Baxter. I live in Austin. I have for years. You can check all that out."

"I know who you are. I know what you've done, and that you did it with that thug right here in this decrepit chunk of metal."

"No. I never lived here. That was Ella. She's in the hospital, recovering from a stab wound. Her boyfriend…"

No. Dani had it all wrong. Kevin hadn't stabbed Ella. This man had, and now he was going to kill her.

The realization sent a new wave of terror coursing through her veins. She had to make him understand that she was not Helena or else break free. She looked around for a weapon and saw one almost immediately.

A pearl-handled dagger rested on the pillows next to a pair of silky pantaloons. It was the weapon he was going to use to kill her.

He let go of her arm and shoved her across the bed. "Put the dress on. Wear it for me the way you wore it for him."

The dress from her nightmarish vision. The dagger that had plunged into her heart. She gagged on the fear. "No. I won't wear it. It's not mine."

"Put on the dress."

She lunged for the dagger. He caught her feet and yanked her back toward him before she could reach it.

His fist hammered against her right cheek, and she fell into the folds of the horrid gown. She tasted blood. She retched and barely kept from being sick.

When she looked up again, he was holding

the dagger in his right hand. He slipped the blade beneath her sweater and twisted the cold tip into her flesh until blood trickled down her abdomen. With a jerk of his hand, he sliced through her sweater and bra from top to bottom.

She used her hands to try and cover herself from his leering gaze as her sweater fell away. He chuckled at her humiliation and slid the blade between her thighs.

"Do you want to take off your jeans by yourself, or should I take care of that for you as well?"

Panic consumed her. This was just the way it had happened in the vision. She couldn't put on the dress, but not doing what he said would get her killed, too.

The shame and terror were all part of his plan, but in the end he would plunge the dagger into her heart just as he had in the nightmare.

She struggled for control as her horror and anger melded into a hard core of resistance.

"I'm not Helena. I've never worn that dress for anyone else, and I won't wear it for you."

Vile curses flew from his mouth, and he exploded into a frenzied rage. His nostrils flared. His hands knotted into hammerlike fists.

Now she understood the fear she'd seen in Ella's eyes.

He punched her in the stomach and yanked the jeans off her body while she regained her equilibrium.

"Don't make me hurt you, my sweet. Put on the dress. I want to see you in it."

His tone turned soothing as if he'd assumed a new personality. A Jekyll and Hyde, monster and gentleman. But if she crossed him, she knew the rage would return. Antagonizing him only brought out the beast. She'd have to appease and then outsmart him.

She reached for the dress and slipped it over her head. Ella was thinner than her and the dress fit tightly, squeezing her waist and pushing her breasts from the wired cups.

"That's so much better, my sweet." He reached beneath the skirt and let his hand slide up her thigh. "I know you made love to him, Helena. Right here on this bed. You'll make love to me the same way."

The man was sick. Life with him had to be pure hell for Ella. He was the opposite of everything good. The antithesis of all she loved about Marcus.

Loved. It was uncanny that the word would slip so easily into her thoughts now. All Marcus had asked for was a chance for them to make it work together. She'd been afraid to even try.

Afraid of failure. Afraid of loving. Afraid of losing.

"I would have made you happy if you'd let me, Helena. You ruined all that." He ran his thumb along the edge of the dagger as seductively as if he were touching a woman's breast.

"I could have been everything to you. Now you've forced me to have to take your life."

Dani became paralyzed by fear. He was going to rape and then kill her. She was going to die, and Celeste would go through life without a mother, the same way Dani had. She'd never even have a chance to tell her goodbye.

She'd never get to know her twin sister, whoever she might be. She wouldn't be there to take care of Grams.

She'd never feel Marcus's lips on hers again. Never thrill to his touch again or wake up in his arms. Or make love with him.

I love you, Marcus. I should have told you that. I should have given us a chance.

Marcus would say to never give up. She wasn't ready to die. One last burst of adrenaline raced through her bloodstream, obliterating the fear that had held her captive. She brought a knee to the monster's crotch in a fierce surge of force.

He cursed and grabbed himself as he stumbled backward. She shoved past him and made a run for it, grabbing her skirt and holding it up to keep from tripping as she raced for the front door. She'd almost reached it when he grabbed her from behind and slung her against the wall. Something cracked and she slid to the floor, dissolving into a puddle of green velvet.

The dagger was poised and ready to strike.

I didn't give up, Marcus. I just lost the war.

Chapter Fifteen

Marcus made the turn into the camping area on two wheels. This was all his fault, and if anything happened to Dani, he'd never forgive himself. He'd sensed the danger to her from the very beginning. He wasn't a psychic, but he did have a sixth sense about that.

The jagged pieces of the puzzle had never really fit. The note at the festival. The snapshot left at the convenience store. Even Dani's trance had all pointed to the fact that she was in jeopardy.

He'd let his emotions file the edges from his wary foreboding and keen sense of impending peril. He'd left the way clear for her to walk directly into the path of a maniac.

He'd been trying to reach her by phone ever since he grabbed Cutter's gun and rushed out of the main house. He wasn't alarmed that she hadn't taken his call. He half expected that she'd avoid talking to him.

He'd prayed she'd read his text message: *Don't go to Ella's trailer. It's a trap!*

He slammed on the breaks and skidded to a stop, inches from Dani's car. There was no other car around. Maybe she was inside by herself, safe, looking for the insurance papers she'd believe the hospital had asked for.

Maybe not.

Adrenaline pumping, he pulled his gun and crashed though the door. The wall in front of him was streaked with blood. Fresh blood, still wet and dripping. Whatever had happened in this room had occurred only moments before he arrived.

The trailer was silent, but that didn't mean that Ethan Marks wasn't here. Marcus's fighting instincts were in full operational mode, his senses razor sharp.

Finger on the trigger, he skulked toward the back of the camper with his back to the wall. Drops of fresh blood lined the hallway floor. A woman's shoe, maybe Dani's, lay in haphazard fashion as if it had been kicked off or knocked from her foot. The matching shoe was approximately two feet away, near the bedroom at the end of the short hall.

A slender, jagged scratch, approximately four feet long and waist high, ran along the opposite wall. His mind took all that in automatically in the few split seconds it took him to reach the closed door.

"Stay back. It's a trap."

Dani's voice. Ella had surmised this right. Her maniac husband had mistaken Dani for her.

Marcus surveyed his options. Open the door to a trap or risk the man's murdering Dani while he tried to figure a new plan. Seconds mattered.

He shoved the door open and went in low, tackling the bastard at the knees and sending him sprawling across the floor and into the closet door. The man slashed at him with a dagger as he went down. Marcus dodged the blow and the point of the blade just grazed his shoulder.

The man backed away, but instead of coming after Marcus again, he thrust the blade beneath Dani's chin, inches from her jugular.

"Do you think your lover will still want you when your head is rolling across the floor, Helena?"

The lowdown, rotten, murderous bastard.

"Kill her, Ethan Marks, and you'll never walk away from here alive."

"Do you think I care? Do you think I want to live without Helena?"

"You care, Ethan. It was never about me. It was always about you and your possessions. I'm not one of those anymore."

Marcus was stunned by the accusations flowing from Dani's mouth even with the blade at her throat. She wasn't Helena, had never been Ethan's wife. What the hell was she doing?

"Look at Marcus, Ethan. He's my real lover. He's had me in and out of this green dress. He's touched me all the places you used to touch me, and I enjoyed it much more. I've made love to him in ways I never made love to you."

Panic swelled in Marcus's chest. "She's not Helena. She's not your wife. She's not my lover."

"He's lying, Ethan."

"Shut up, Helena," Ethan ordered.

"No, I won't shut up. You used to order me around, but not anymore. Look at Marcus, Ethan. See what a real man looks like."

Ethan yanked the dagger from her throat and held it high above her head, ready to plunge it deep into her chest. Marcus fired twice, both bullets hitting their mark. The dagger fell from the man's bloody fingers, and the blade impaled his right foot to the floor.

He screamed in agony.

The front door burst open, and Cutter came running down the hall. Marcus crossed the crowded room in an instant and pulled Dani into his arms. Nothing in his life had ever felt so good.

"Are you all right?"

"A little bloody and battered. Nothing serious. How did you know Ethan was here?"

"A long story. You have Ella to thank."

"If you hadn't shown up when you did, I'd be dead."

"I thought you were going to be anyway when you started channeling Helena."

"I wasn't channeling. I just trusted the vision and those special ops skills of yours."

"The vision that left you dead?"

"By a dagger in the heart, not a slashed throat. I knew when he tried to stab me you'd shoot him and it would all be over. Well, I didn't know it, but I was sure counting on it working on that way."

He held her against him. "God bless the visions."

"I love you, Marcus."

He couldn't believe his ears.

"You guys really know how to wreck a trailer," Cutter said. "But I'd say a dagger beats handcuffs for confining criminals, hands down."

"You should call for an ambulance for him," Dani said.

"I'll leave that up to the sheriff. He should be walking through the front door just about…now."

The sheriff entered on cue. Cutter explained the little he knew of the situation to him, basically what he'd been told by Linney as he'd rushed from the house a few minutes behind Marcus.

Marcus went back to the business at hand. He nudged a thumb under Dani's chin and tilted it up so that he could look into her eyes. "What did you say a minute ago?"

"About the ambulance?"

"A sentence before that."

"I love you. I just thought you should know in case you're still game to give us a chance."

His heart swelled to the size of a watermelon. "Smart move on your part. With your penchant for trouble, you could go broke if you had to hire me every time you needed my help."

"I don't recall firing you yet. So take me home, cowboy, and show me what else you've got in your special ops bag of tricks."

He grinned from the inside out. "Baby, you ain't seen nothing yet!"

Epilogue

Two months later

Dani adjusted her sun visor as the road curved to the west. It was three o'clock on a warm, sunny afternoon in mid-December. Marcus had insisted they go for a ride after they'd finished with Grams's birthday celebration at the nursing home, but he'd been unusually silent for most of it.

She'd tried to make conversation several times but gotten nowhere. Whatever was on his mind, he clearly wasn't ready to talk about it.

"Thanks for helping with the party," she said, giving communication another chance.

"All I did was dish up the chocolate mint ice cream."

"And charm every female in the place from ages twelve to a hundred, especially Grams."

"She was definitely in good spirits for a woman turning ninety-six."

"And has been ever since she was reunited with her long-lost no-name granddaughter," Dani reflected. "It makes me wonder how much psychic knowledge she had about Helena through the years."

"Hopefully enough to know Helena had a great childhood and graduated from Tulane at the top of her class. That is what Helena said, isn't it?"

"Right, a great life until the car wreck where both her adoptive parents were killed and she ended up in a lengthy fight for her life. That accident correlates with Grams's first stroke. I think the two must be related."

"But the stroke left your grandmother too mentally and physically disabled to go to Helena. That makes sense," Marcus admitted. "How long did you say Helena was in the coma?"

"Almost six months, long enough to go through every penny of her inheritance, at least that was what Ethan had her believe. It turns out even that wasn't true."

"Really? I haven't heard this."

"A new development that's come out in the prosecutor's investigation. Ethan was not only a psychopath but a crooked attorney who hooked up with Helena when she was at her most vulnerable, swindled her out of over a million dollars and then lured her into marriage so she wouldn't figure it all out."

"Maybe he loved her in his own sick way," Marcus said.

"Extremely sick, and I don't think it classifies as love."

"Guess you're right." Marcus made another turn, this one heading south through beautiful hill country ranchland. "I'm just thankful it all turned out the way it did."

"More thanks to you. I'm alive and have a twin sister who I already love. She's moving into her own apartment next week. It's only a few blocks from the house, but I know I'll miss her terribly."

Marcus tugged his Stetson a bit lower on his forehead. "Yeah. Missing someone can be tough."

The comment served to dismiss the topic. Marcus grew quiet again, and a tense uneasiness settled between them. It was the first weekend they'd had together in three weeks. She'd missed him so much she could barely stand it, and now that he was here, he was closing her out.

Finally she could stand it no longer. "If something is wrong, Marcus, just say it."

"Okay. Give me another minute or two."

More silence to grate along her nerves.

Finally, he pulled off the blacktop road and clattered over a cattle gap and through an open gate. "Let's get out," he said.

She did and met him at the front of his truck, suddenly so nervous she could barely swallow. If this was going to be a swan dance, she didn't think she could take it. Not now. Not after she'd given her heart so totally to him.

He leaned his backside against the truck's hood. "I thought I could make this work, Dani, but this long-distance relationship isn't cutting it for me."

Her insides knotted. "I know we've both been busy, but it won't always be like this."

"Yeah, Dani. It will be. My job is not a five-days-a-week operation. Your job is demanding and Celeste has school, so weekends and a few vacation days are all you have."

She swallowed hard. The one man she'd thought was different. The one who'd said he never gave up. "So what does this mean?"

"Cutter planned to have Hawk open a field office when he signs on with us next week. I asked him to give that option to me, and he's agreed."

Would she never learn? "So you'll be moving away from Dobbin?"

"It looks that way."

"Where will you go?"

"Austin, at least part of the time."

Her pulse revved up a notch or two. "Austin, with all its traffic and congestion?"

"Could be. I'm not much on waiting around for things to fall into place, Dani. I'm a grab-the-bull-by-the-horns kind of guy. So here goes."

He stepped in front of her and took both her hands in his, then fell to his knees. "Marry me, Dani. Now. Tomorrow. I'll even wait until next week if you like. But I don't need time to know that I want you in my life forever, and we're wasting precious time we could be together."

A million reasons why she should say no stormed her mind. One reason for saying yes claimed control. "I love you, Marcus Abbot, with all my heart."

"Is that a yes?"

"That would be a yes."

He rummaged in his pocket and pulled out a simple gold ring with a dazzling, solitaire diamond. "I love you, Dani. I have since the moment I met you. I always will."

He slipped the ring on her finger, then stood and pulled her into his arms.

Her heart overflowed, but still she couldn't push back all the worries. "My house is big enough for all of us, but how will you endure the city?"

"Because I know that time off we'll have this, a mere forty-five minutes away."

"A drive in the country won't be the same as living on the Double M."

"That's why I plan to build a house on the land and a barn for the horses Celeste wants."

"Wait. Whose ranch is this?"

"Soon to be *ours.* Cutter's doing the financing. I sign the papers tomorrow—unless you'd said no. I was counting on your not saying no."

Slowly it was all sinking in. God, she loved him, just the way he was. "Cocky, aren't you?"

"Yep." He flashed the devastating smile that always turned her inside out.

"I can't wait to explore the ranch."

"It's small, but big enough. And it has this great little stream with the perfect pine-straw carpeted spot for making love."

"So why are we still standing here?"

"And I thought I was the one who loved action." He held her close and kissed her—a long, sweet wet kiss that held a lifetime of promise.

This time there were no worries. When a woman found the perfect cowboy, it was best not to question fate but just to grab the reins and hold on. It didn't take a psychic to know that.

* * * * *